THE GRUNGE OPERATIVES

ALSO BY AARON HILTON
Skin Deep Motives

THE GRUNGE OPERATIVES

A NOVEL

AARON HILTON

PORTLAND, OREGON

A BACKWATER CRIME BOOK

First Paperback Edition: August 2016

Copyright © 2016 by Aaron Hilton

Edited by Alex Hurst
Cover Art by Carl Graves
Illustrations & Logo by Daniel Cooney

ISBN 978-0-9853941-5-8

This is for my wife, Kim.
Surrendering many nights so that my
imagination can soar.

THE GRUNGE OPERATIVES

ONE

Leslie Crow

Breathing deeply, I managed the pain and restrained my excitement for my finished ink. I'd been sitting backwards, draped on the tattoo chair since late morning with only a couple of short breaks in-between. I glanced up at the antique Dutch clock mounted above a Vargas Girl pin-up calendar. The metallic cogs and gears clacked as a wooden finch poked out to chirp and whistle *cuckoo-cuckoo* seven times. The buzz of the tattoo machine and the burning back massage from the stinging needles ended.

"Okay," Daniil Sokolov stood up, "all done. How are you doing, Leslie? Can I refill your water? Some hot tea maybe?"

"No, Daniil, I'm good."

"Rest here for a little while," he said. "I'm stepping outside for a smoke."

I allowed myself a brief grin. His tone, augmented

by a rich Ukrainian accent, sounded as fulfilled as a lover's post coitus. I'd made a wise decision in tracking down Dee's mentor to color her last back piece.

My iPhone vibrated. Unclipping the handset, I checked the display to read: Matt.

"What?" I answered.

I concentrated to hear over the heavy metal music blaring in the background.

"Hey, partner," Matt shouted, "you hadn't checked into the hotel yet, so I wanted to make sure everything's cool."

"Matt, I'm on vacation . . ." I bit my tongue before I could call him an asshole.

"Working vacation. What's wrong, Leslie?"

"Nothing," I said. "I arrived a few days early to take care of personal things and I don't need you looming."

"Hey Matt," a girl's low-pitched, sultry voice called out, "I'm taking a break. In fifteen minutes I'll give you that lap dance."

"Two songs, or three?" he said, then came back to me. "What's that, Leslie? Where were we?"

He sure sounded chipper for a private detective whose fuck buddy had recently set him up, then left him beaten, tortured, handcuffed and hanging from a meathook. The fantastic healing powers of strip joints.

"I'll check in with you in two days," I said. "Then you can brag about how many stripper bars you staked out to get a lead on Alec Winter."

"Gentleman clubs," he corrected.

"Don't quibble with me, Matt."

"I'm not trying to. You know how many clubs operate here. But so far, I can't complain about the . . . fringe benefits of this case."

"Oh, *brother* . . . Remember what happened with Pepper, Matt. I think you'll do better if you just admire the menu and keep your dick in your pants."

I ended the call and turned my phone off.

By the fresh aroma of nicotine I smelled, Daniil had returned.

I inhaled the lemongrass scent of the sanitizer he washed his hands with. He snapped on a fresh pair of Latex gloves. The flicker of the flashbulb lit our shadows up on the wall. I heard the shutter click of an old school Polaroid camera and the slide mechanism eject the film.

I turned my head right ninety-degrees. The sharp movement was a little too quick after relaxing backwards on a chair for several hours. The vertebrae in my neck cracked.

"Ouch."

As Daniil fanned the picture in one hand, his other hand clutched the back of my neck and stroked it firmly.

Oh. My. God. I moaned. He stopped squeezing. I heard him peel the positive from the negative.

"Here," Daniil said, handing me the photograph. "Take a look. Not bad for an old man, huh?"

I pinched the photo of my back piece and scrutinized Dee's final masterpiece in vivid color. My eyes widened. The last time colors had tapped into my senses so magically I was four. I'd caught a glimpse on a color TV through a storefront window in a town off the reservation. Judy Garland was stepping foot into Oz.

No one on the res owned a color TV in the late seventies. I'd wanted to just stand there in the freezing winter chill and watch a little more, but my mom hurried me along, pointing at the sign in the window that'd read *No Indians or Loitering*.

I racked my vocabulary, searching for the right words to convey my feelings.

"I wish Dee and my mom were still alive to see this," I finally said.

"How did your mom die, Leslie?"

"Thanks for asking. I appreciate it. I really do. But I'm feeling too much bliss right now to kill the mood. Some other time."

"I'm going to bandage you up now, then. I figure that with all your other tats, I don't have to remind you about after-care to stave off infection."

"No, but each one has healed differently. Go ahead and give me a refresher."

"For starters, I'm going to relieve the swelling," he said.

A squeeze bottle gurgled, then alcohol trickled down my back. The cool liquid tamed the heat. After rubbing the alcohol in with his strong hands, Daniil applied a generous coat of Vaseline. Next, I heard the sheets of plastic wrap he tore off, before he affixed them to my back with medical tape.

"Leave this bandage on for two-to-twelve hours. Wash your hands before removing it. Take the bandage off slowly. If it won't come off easily, don't pull—moisten the bandage with warm water instead. In the shower is best. Don't soak the tattoo. Don't scrub or use a washcloth. Gently work off anything on the surface with your hands. Pat it dry, never rub it. Wear something that breathes. Cotton's good. No nylon or polyester. Also, try to avoid any hard workouts that flex the tattoo or cause excessive perspiration. Keep the tattoo moist over the next several days with Curel or Lubriderm."

"Okay," I said.

"Do you have something else you can wear other than the T-shirt you came in with?"

"In my messenger bag," I told him.

After retrieving it for me, Daniil waited in the outer room. I got up out of the chair and stood still for a moment to keep my legs from cramping up. I reached into the bag.

Forgoing the restraint and push of a bra, I pulled out a sleeveless satin blouse and pulled the wispy, red garment on over my torso. I left the two bottom buttons undone to parade my abs, rising phoenix tat, and pierced naval. A friend once told me my outie was my sexiest feature and that I should show it off as often as possible.

I pulled the messenger bag up over my shoulder. The curtain of beads rattled as I parted them to enter the main room. Daniil was sitting in a straight-back chair, holding the heart-shaped box I'd delivered, trails of tears staining his cheeks. He got up quickly. Setting Dee's ashes down on the counter by the cash register, he wiped his eyes off with the cuff of his corduroy shirt.

"Daniil, do you want me to hang out for a while longer? You shouldn't be alone right now."

"Nah, being able to finish Dee's vision has helped with the grieving process. My boyfriend will return from work within the hour. I'll be alright."

"Okay. I'll see you in a couple days for Dee's funeral."

"Where are you staying?"

"The Sheraton at Fisherman's Wharf," I said.

"Isn't that a little touristy for a P.I.?"

Oh no, what kind of hotel did Matt book me into?

"I'll check in with you tomorrow night. Call me if you need any help with the funeral arrangements, or if you just need to talk."

"Sure. Take care of that tattoo, Leslie."

"Thanks. Goodnight." I actually smiled, then walked out of the Boogie Clay Crafts and Gifts head shop.

A chilly breeze brushed against my exposed skin and sprouted goosebumps. Pulling my leather jacket on, I stowed my messenger bag in one of the storage pods on the back of my motorcycle. I glanced left and right.

Across the street, a pair of twenty-something guys were walking and holding hands. The younger man held a leash in his clenched fist.

I turned and headed right, on a parallel course with the boys.

Their white and brown dog bounded up the

sidewalk, pausing only to sniff a garbage can and a fire hydrant. The dog barked and leapt ahead, jerking his owner's right arm upward. The leash handle clicked to feed the rambunctious canine a little more line.

"Archie," the young man strong-arming the leash said, "slow down, boy."

The mutt panted rapidly and wagged his tail in response. He barked again.

I mounted my motorcycle. Donning my helmet, I planted my feet firmly on the asphalt to balance the bike, then swiveled the kickstand up with my riding boot heel. I stomped the engine on. It vibrated steadily against my thighs.

A good memory rushed to my head. My first date when I was sixteen had showed up on a motorcycle. We'd sped around San Francisco for hours. Arms wrapped around him tight, I kept screaming, "Faster!"

Putting the Streetfighter in gear, I looked behind me in both directions, and slowly backed out. I liked to think that I'd outgrown being a reckless teenager a long time ago.

Since my body was still consumed by endorphins and adrenaline, I didn't go to the hotel right away. In two days my vacation would be over and the paying case that'd brought me to the Bay would require several exhaustive hours of surveillance. I needed to know my way around.

I toured the districts of San Francisco. Having lived here in my youth, reorienting my directional senses didn't take much time. The traffic lights switching to yellow or red did, though.

I resigned myself to admiring the mishmash of architecture and cultures: a lush green park with clean playground equipment and basketball courts sandwiched in between suburban houses; medium-sized condominiums rising up out of pubs, clothing shops, or hand-made jewelry boutiques; the gaudy blue and pink neon marquee of The Castro Theater that read *Bogie Film Festival* beginning with *The Petrified Forrest* and *Jerry Goldsmith Tribute featuring Chinatown*.

I didn't know either one of those movies.

A trio of drag queens, colorful peacock feathers highlighting their bouffant hairdos and high heels click-clacking, negotiated a trip down a steep flight of stone steps in front of a tall Victorian house with gingerbread trim. They moved with more grace than I would've ever been able to pull off in a pair of those damn things. A hand-carved wooden sign staked in the grass beside the stairs read *Tommie's Bed & Breakfast: Free Wi-Fi*. The vibrant red neon Vacancy sign glowed like a beacon.

Cholos cruising in a lowrider pulled out in front of me on Mission Street. I squeezed the brakes hard. The sudden stop jostled the Streetfighter and jerked my body forward. The curse I hurled was absorbed by the live salsa music blasting from a nearby cantina.

Spicy aromas of grilled meats and vegetables drifting around the strip flooded the vents of my helmet and made me salivate. My stomach rumbled. The last time I'd eaten was around noon. Daniil had ordered a late lunch delivery from Orphan Andy's. I'd devoured a creamy tuna and sharp cheddar melt piled with sliced red onions and tomatoes on lightly-toasted dark rye.

I licked my lips. It wasn't from hunger, though. Unwilling to be stuck behind a street gang cruising the town, I spot-checked oncoming traffic, then made a split-second left turn onto a side street. Motorists forced to stop leaned on their horns.

Whipping past some of the colorful murals for which the Mission District is famous, I hung a right onto Church Street. At Seventeenth Street, I coasted to a smooth stop. The Mission District's namesake and San Francisco's oldest building, Mission Dolores, loomed ahead.

Crossing over to Guerrero, I sped five blocks north up to Market Street and hung another right. Once I hit the Embarcadero traffic thinned out. As I cruised closer to the Bay, I inhaled salty air.

I checked the Honda's fuel gauge. The needle pointed at about a quarter full. A Chevron Station sign glowed up ahead. I swung into the lot and pulled up to the pump. As I listened to the petroleum flow through the nozzle and watched the numbers on the meter flicker, I looked around.

A silver Blazer full of noisy twenty-something guys arguing over what brand of beer to pick up stopped bickering to ogle a foursome of college cheerleaders that rolled up in a jeep. Pop music blaring from their speakers and subwoofer polluted the atmosphere. The girls hip-walked in unison toward the convenience store entrance.

A tall guy, his long albino hair tied back in a ponytail, was washing the windshield of his black Charger.

He was watching me. Our eyes met; not in a cordial manner. His predatory gaze faced front, gauging the distance to his prey. My instincts told me that I'd just been marked.

That intimidation shit didn't work on me.

At the impressionable age of ten, I had stared down a rabid coyote. My dog's blood was dripping from its muzzle and growling fangs. As the drooling beast leapt at me, I had shot an arrow right through its heart.

The albino relented and turned back to his car. Finished with the squeegee, he placed it back in the bucket (careful not to splash any dirty water on his suit), then pumped a few squirts of hand sanitizer on his palms. I noticed he wasn't getting any gas.

"Asshole," one of the cheerleaders hollered.

A bald-headed fella, stocky but muscular, wearing a suit and a tie, nudged the girls out of his path. He stuffed a pack of cigarettes in his front pocket.

Ponytail's lip curled up before he hurled foreign words at his associate. Then the tall albino nodded with a rapid jerk of his V-shaped chin. The angry gesture could've been aimed at the passenger door of their car, or at me.

The pump clicked and a computerized voice

thanked me for my purchase. Getting back on the blue and silver chassis, I started the ignition, then wheeled over to the exit. Oncoming traffic made me wait. I saw the Charger's gleaming windshield pull up behind me in my side mirrors.

I turned left onto Embarcadero and headed north. So did the Charger.

Coming up on Pier 39, the air grew thick with the stench of dumped frier oil from battered seafood. Stomach growling, I thought about my mom's fry bread.

I saw Alcatraz Island. The prison's bleached structure resembled a tomb. Paiutes, Papagoes, Apaches, Shoshones, Modocs, Hopis—long before Al Capone or "the Birdman of Alcatraz" made the Rock famous— were sentenced to the dungeons below the cell block. In the case of a few Hopi prisoners in the 1890s, their crimes were no worse than refusing to surrender their children to missionary boarding schools. Their spirit to preserve their identity was smothered, confined in holes of solid rock where no light could reach.

In 1969, Richard Oakes and Adam Nordwall launched an incursion of the island. American Indians from Nations all over the country made the journey to join the occupation, eager to participate in the rise of traditional Indian consciousness and activism. Being an AIM (American Indian Movement) supporter, my mother, Mina Crow Bear, was one of them. She got pregnant with me—either somewhere in San Francisco or on the Rock after she made landfall—and hoped that

I'd be the first baby born there. Tragically, on a January morning in 1970, the mysterious death of a thirteen-year-old girl, Yvonne—Richard Oakes' daughter, scared my mom. She fled back to the res.

Two vehicles back, the Charger's bright headlights still followed.

I told myself to be cool. My parking angel gave me a spot to pull in a block away from the Sheraton. The Charger parallel parked in a *Customers Only* space for an IHOP. Booths near the window featured a lengthy view of the street and my hotel. They didn't climb out of their car.

Walking up the driveway that separated the hotel's lodgings, I entered the lobby foyer through sliding doors. The posh atmosphere catered to the average business person or family on vacation. American food sizzled in the restaurant on the fringes of the lobby to my left. I walked purposefully to the check-in desk and signed in. The clerk handed over my keycard and wished me a nice stay. She emphasized that my room was located across the way in the brand new wing, closer to the gymnasium and the swimming pool for my convenience.

I inserted the card into the reader slot. The second the mechanism's light switched to green and the lock clicked to release, I pushed the door open and flipped the lights on. My facial muscles drooped with disappointment. Pastel blues, pinks, and yellows brightened the room. The basic amenities didn't include a refrigerator. Fuck, no. This would not do.

I checked out and got back on my Streetfighter. Gunning the engine, I swung out onto the street and the Charger pulled out to follow me from a distance once more. Daniil had been right. I pulled into the parking garage of a Safeway a block away. The assholes in the Charger pulled into a spot just a few spaces away from me.

I bopped into the grocery store. The clicking of my steel riding boots on the slanted concrete echoed throughout the structure.

Grabbing a basket, I placed it in the crook of my arm. I moseyed into the produce department. I gently squeezed a few avocados in my hand for ripeness. Out of the corner of my eye, I saw my follower's elongated shadows proceed their shapes through the sliders.

They split up. The squat one headed for the coolers on the opposite end of the store, while Ponytail stood at an end cap juice display. He snatched a mango smoothie.

I headed over to the perishable veggies. Thunder clapped through the speakers overhead and water jets began to spray a mist. I grabbed a small bunch of cilantro and bagging it, tossed the leafy greens in the basket next to the avocado and a squeeze bottle of lime juice. Wiping my hand off on my thigh, I hipped it slowly to the back of the department and continued on to the next aisles.

In the ethnic foods section I snatched a bottle of Sriracha. In my peripheral vision, I saw Ponytail grab a can of refried beans. I walked towards him. He acted like

I no longer existed. Even when I stood right beside him and stooped forward, accentuating my toned curves a little, to select a can of organic black beans.

I walked around him.

Strolling up the cooking aisle, I grabbed a travel-sized set of sea salt and pepper shakers. The next aisle over I got a pouch of microwavable brown rice, then kept moving.

Ponytail stepped right in my path, the front of his body perfectly open. I bumped into him. While pressing against his chest with my free hand to brace myself, I rammed his balls up into his body cavity with my knee.

Releasing his items, which bounced off the scuffed linoleum floor, Ponytail dropped to his knees, clutching his testicles with both hands. A pair of clerks rushed over to offer help. He wagged his head no.

I sidestepped and made my way to the kitchen aid products section. I picked out a set of disposable plastic containers and a box of utensils. Lastly, I remembered that bottle of Lubriderm.

All done shopping, I went through the express line. As the checker handed me my bagged groceries and wished me goodnight, I noticed Ponytail's partner, Q Ball, had finally caught up with his accomplice and was trying to help him stand up enough to walk.

Heading for the main entry sliders, I stopped by the boxed displays of candy bars to open my plastic bag in shock.

"Shit! I forgot to grab *Inked*."

I swung around and headed for the periodicals. Q Ball patted Ponytail on the shoulder, then followed after me to intercept.

A gap separated the paperbacks from the magazines. I darted through it and hustled to the rear of the store. I pushed out the emergency exit in the foyer between the pharmacy and the row of dairy cases.

Q Ball entered the area. Clasping palms over his ears to mute the shrieking alarm that emanated from the speaker on the crash bar, Q Ball nudged the door open. He took two steps outside.

Springing up from a crouch near the aspirin shelves in his blind spot, I drove a side kick into Q Ball's hip. He slammed into the asphalt. I pulled the door shut. To get back inside he'd have to traverse a trip around the entire block.

I jogged up to the front of the store, mindful of any clerks rushing to the back to check on the alarm. I grinned. It seemed that all the other customers had chosen that particular moment to swarm into the register lanes. As I dashed through the sliders, I could hear management over the PA system calling all checkers for assistance.

Stashing my sack of groceries in one of the pods on the back of my bike, I hopped onto the seat, strapped my helmet on, stomped the engine into a roar, and sped away from the wharf.

Now that my unwanted appendage wasn't around, I could figure out a safe place to stay. I recalled that another one of my girlfriends from my teen years was staying in San Francisco.

Ali lived in one of those brand new, sheik condos that'd sprouted up in Haight-Ashbury. This hip district reminded me of Hawthorne or the Pearl in Portland. A neighborhood for second-generation hippies, struggling artists, and pot enthusiasts.

I parked in a loading zone between her building and a pawn shop. Trudging uphill to the front stoop, I ran my finger over the call buttons until I zeroed in on Ali's number. The name tag above the buzzer was gone. I double-checked the address. No, I had it right. Ali had moved without staying in touch with me. *Well that sneaky bitch . . .*

What other option did I have for a place to stay? Then I remembered the bed and breakfast in the Castro I'd seen.

●

From the moment I walked inside the Victorian's parlor, an atmosphere laden with incense and solid wood furnishings enveloped me with warmth.

My upstairs room at the end of the hall featured a queen-size bed, a compact fridge that contained an honor bar, a microwave, a bathroom with a cast iron tub, and a detachable shower head. An oasis to an urban Indian like me.

I unpacked my clothes and stored them in the meticulously sanded and varnished maple chest of drawers across from the foot of the bed. On the right side of the bed near the door I pulled my boots off and stretched my toes. I padded into the bathroom to wash the streets off my hands.

Sliding my iPad out of my satchel, I set the case stand up on the walnut-lacquered nightstand. I tapped the Music icon and selected an Enigma playlist to help me relax.

As the monks began to cantillate, I popped the pouch of rice in the microwave for ninety-seconds. I used the can opener on my Leatherman tool to pry open the can of beans, then drained them in the bathroom sink. When the microwave timer dinged, I was cutting the avocado in two.

I dumped half the rice into one of the disposable bowls, dashed a little salt, twisted some pepper, then fluffed it with a fork. Spooning black beans on, I topped it with the avocado flesh, cilantro sprigs, and hot sauce shaken on like a maraca. Meatless Monday dinner was served.

Sitting down cross-legged at the head of the bed, I swiveled the tablet around. I took a bite of my simple meal and connected to the streaming Wi-Fi. Browsing blogs and news sites for Portland to keep up on current events, I discovered a headline interesting enough to read aloud with my mouth full.

"Can't Beat a Classic: Premier Detective Wildly Apprehends Strangler Suspect, Driving Bullitt Mustang."

TWO

Matt Grudge

In Oregon strippers take *everything* off. Gyrating to Wilson Pickett's *Mustang Sally*, Medusa slowly thumbed the lacy waistband of her fire engine red panties down. The curly-haired brunette strutted passed the three guys sitting at the half moon-shaped stage. Her black platform heels agilely stepped around beer bottles and rock glasses.

The small round table I was sitting at afforded me a decent view of the show. I tipped the rim of my pint glass to my lips. The smooth amber brew with a squeeze of fresh lemon flowed down my throat. I needed it. Beads of sweat moistened my neck and armpits. No one else in the place seemed to be uncomfortable from the heat.

There weren't too many bodies inside either. Maybe I was fighting a bug.

Kneeling down, Medusa crawled along the countertop. Her glossy black lips puckered up, blowing singles out of her path.

She leapt upward. Clutching the jungle gym bars riveted between the ceiling rafters, Medusa shifted around, swung up, hooked her ankles in, and then hung upside down. The silken strands of the silver streaks in her hair flailed in gravity like an orgy of serpents. Her eager spectators tossed more bills. She ran a hand up her torso, massaged her tanned breasts.

Unhooking one leg and still holding on with only one arm, Medusa used her free hand to slide her red hot panties mid-thigh. She wriggled and shimmied until they dangled from her ankle.

Medusa snatched the garment. Pulling the tight elastic back with her teeth, she aimed and launched them through the red-tinted atmosphere. A businessman dribbled neat whiskey down his loosened tie, laughing. The panties touched down to drape over the front brim of his gray fedora.

Releasing the bars, Medusa landed on both feet. She swung her hips to the furious bass of Rob Zombie's *Spookshow Baby*.

I snatched a tortilla chip from the edge of my plate. Dipping it in oozy nacho cheese sauce and sour cream, I scooped up a few chunks of over-cooked beef, jalapeños, and olives before jamming the bite into my mouth.

The industrial metal with a touch of boogie-woogie came to an abrupt finish. The audience clapped and whistled. Medusa picked up her tips. On her way off the stage, she grabbed her panties from the businessman's hat to pull them up her long legs. He tilted the brim up cordially and swung around to talk to Medusa.

I scooted my chair around. Peering over the rim of my perspiring glass, I practiced a little lip reading. The place was small, intimate, and not too crowded, yet.

"That was some fine dancing," Fedora said. "Buy you a drink?"

"Stick around, maybe later," she said. "If I don't take my lunch now, I'll never get it."

"Wait a minute, doll. Wouldn't a little conversation and refreshment go nice with your break?"

Medusa chuckled, strapping her bra on. "You really want to sex me up as I call my sitter to check in on my kid?"

The next dancer bounced up onto the stage. Two more fellas sat down. Their heads followed the new arrival like a pointer scenting game. The businessman followed suit.

"Didn't think so," Medusa said.

She turned around. Stuffing her tips down her cleavage, Medusa made her way towards a large table between the path that lead to the main entrance and the bar, with a short row of video gambling machines blinking and chirping just on the other side. She negotiated a path through some tables, then stopped at the water cooler by the door to get a cup of ice water.

Pulling out a flip phone concealed in a pouch on the side of her bra, Medusa hit a number in her speed dial. Her facial expression went from being all business and seductive to the glowing love of a mother.

"Hey, Little Man. Yes, I'm working. You need to speak up so I can hear you. No, Mommy won't think you're yelling. You want to watch what? . . . *It's the Great Pumpkin, Charlie Brown*. Sing me the ABC Song and you can . . ."

A couple minutes (and only one correction) later, a misty-eyed Medusa closed her phone, replaced it in its garment holster, and finished making her way to that larger table. The sound system sat on top of it, and all of the strippers on shift congregated there also.

"My son just sang me the alphabet," she cheered over The Mammas and the Papas' *California Dreamin'*, and gave one of her co-workers a hug.

I panned right. The five patrons perched on the stools at the bar since I'd entered an hour ago were still there. An auburn-haired young woman was texting on her phone, a mug of coffee and a thick textbook opened by her elbow. Three middle-aged men with potbellies and graying hair seemed to be more taken in by the liquor in their glasses than the girls baring their assets.

A hot blonde on the end in a U of O tank top that barely contained her bombshell figure applauded over her head, then whistled, using her fingers to raise the pitch. It was 'New Yorker hailing a cab' loud. Her spirit was infectious. I ogled her toned legs in too-tight bleached jeans. Her flats were hooked into the legs of the stool.

An arc of fading daylight penetrating the smoldering red atmosphere whipped my focus back to the main entrance. I'd almost turned fast and hard enough to give myself whiplash. It was a tell in my surveillance technique I needed to work on. Granted most people in any strip joint were too enthralled by nude girls to pay any attention to the thirty-something "habitual" customer with sandy blond hair cut Marine-style, a frayed black T-shirt featuring a *Parental Advisory* warning, slashed jeans, and blue Doc Martens. But even the most ordinary guy in the room could blow his cover looking too eager.

Half-a-dozen teenage boys ambled inside. Their acne and their goggling eyes darting to the stripper on the stage betrayed they were minors. The lady bartender, doubling as a bouncer, carded them promptly and eighty-sixed the bunch.

I really wanted Alec Winter to show so I could wrap up this case and move on.

Five years ago, the software designer hit multiple covers of financial magazines, and the publicity machine behind his rising celebrity compared him to Bill Gates and Quentin Tarantino. Then, three years ago his wife arrived home early on his birthday to plan a surprise party to find his dick in an Asian immigrant. His wife was three months pregnant.

Odd as it may seem, pictures of his now ex-wife, Stacie (no maiden name), or their child had never been published. Winter must've paid off the media or hired tight security to keep his failed marriage and offspring that confidential.

I fingered through a few more bites of my nacho platter. It'd sat too long and the smothered chips had become limp and mushy. I polished off my beer. Grabbing my leather jacket off the back of the chair, I left the Lucky Devil Lounge.

I walked beneath the trim of awning and looked around the parking lot. Police cruisers wouldn't begin their stakeouts for DUI violators until closer to midnight. I paused climbing into Leslie's midnight blue Saturn LX, wondering who owned the Mustang a few spots nearby.

I turned the engine over. Colder weather gave it a subtle rattle. Thick raindrops were bombarding the windshield, so I turned the wipers on low. Backing out, I drove left onto Powell and headed east. Nighttime rush hour was thinning out and made cruising up the boulevard smoother. I passed the Aladdin Theatre on my right, then beyond the train tracks on the overpass, Cleveland Park and the high school of the same name. The odor of French fries between two competing fast food restaurants across from each other tugged at my senses.

They both lost to the Safari Club's marquee that proclaimed *T-bone Tuesday $5.99* and *Strippers Are People Too*.

I didn't stop there though. I'd spent three hours in that gentleman's club last night. The deejay that played more hip-hop than I could tolerate wasn't my issue with returning. It was the girls who really knew how to ply their trade. By socializing with patrons between dance sets, they were very convincing at getting customers to follow them into a private booth for a lap dance, which cost anywhere from thirty-to-fifty-dollars a pop, and were usually limited to two songs, sometimes only one. Rates varied place-to-place, depending on the girl's confidence, experience, and how much of a stage fee the establishment charged them to perform.

Envisioning my mark and the obscene amounts of cash a software developer could afford to throw around, I could see Winter prowling strip joints. And from the testimonials of my clients, he had a sweet tooth for strippers. They were drawn to his money. It would be like a fisherman using dynamite.

I opted to try Blush at the bottom of the hill, a shack that shared space in an oblong square with a Chinese food restaurant and an Original Taco House.

Pulling into a parking spot, I watched the back door of the shack open. Two dancers wearing transparent, hooded raincoats over their colorful lingerie and skinny legs were taking a smoke break with a burly, steroid-sized bouncer. The red cherry tips of their cigarettes lit up the bleak shroud of night.

I reached into the backseat for my gym bag. Unzipping the main compartment, I withdrew a folded

Hawaiian button-down shirt. I shook the silk fabric loose to get some of the wrinkles out. Removing my jacket, I pulled my T-shirt up over my head, then pulled the fresh threads on. I tossed the T-shirt in the bag. After fastening the bamboo buttons, I pulled my jacket back on, got out of the car and walked over to Blush.

Hearing an engine purr, I turned to see the Mustang from before pull into the lot. The hot blonde stepped out. The pouring rain drenched her tank top. Her chilled nipples poked through the cotton. She ignored my staring and splashed through water puddles, trotting into the Mexican restaurant.

I shook off seeing her again as a coincidence. Portland is a small city.

As I walked a wide path around the shack to the front entrance on Powell, I could still smell the menthol and tar carried on the east winds. I roamed inside. The girls on the single stage weren't really dancing. It was an exhibition of flesh and girl-on-girl fantasy. In my book, the decorator got extra points, though. The legendary portrait of Marilyn Monroe dabbing Chanel No. 5 on her cleavage was hanging on the wall behind the bar between oak shelves of liquor.

I scoped out the specials on the menu. The low light and small print made the items and prices hard to decipher. Although putting on a pair of cheap reading glasses reminded me that I missed the youth of my twenties, at least they added a new dimension to my disguise.

I ordered a rum and Coke. The busty Latina bartender wore her hair in dreadlocks down to her hips. Bulging, bold lettering across her rack read *Tipping Is Sexy*. After staring at her hands juggling the bottle and glass to pour my drink, I obliged and dropped a sawbuck in the fish bowl by the register.

I slouched to get comfortable, sitting at a table with my back to the wall. With the stage in the center of the joint facing me, I could monitor the front and rear entrance in my peripheral vision. They both opened in unison. A patron came in through the front, while the girls and their bouncer chaperon milled back inside.

The new customer wasn't Winter. Shit.

I sat through three more sets (two songs each) of shimmying and shaking bods. The flooring, tables, soles of my boots, and my ribcage pulsated from a playlist of mullet rock. Would it have killed the place to play a little alternative or punk? I was beginning to wonder if Leslie kept any aspirins in the glovebox of the Saturn. My ears were ringing and my head throbbed every time I shifted my eyes.

My chest was vibrating even though the music paused for a minute.

Then I remembered stowing my Android phone in my left jacket pocket. I plucked it out and checked the caller I.D. *Unknown Caller* flashed. I had a hunch it was the mysterious triumvirate of women who'd approached Alternative Investigations for this job.

Getting up, I stepped out back for a little privacy

and some quiet. The coast was clear and the rain had stopped. I took the call through the Bluetooth clipped to my ear. "Yeah, hello."

"Did you find him yet?" Star O'Hara said.

She couldn't have been using a better alias unless her parents were former hippies. I strained to hear anything in the background that may've given away her true identity or location, but all I picked up was the timid vibe of her voice.

"We're running out of time," she added. "Stacie and her son are days away from being thrown out on the streets."

"Nope, I haven't found him yet," I said.

A short beep on the line indicated that one of the other clients conferenced in to join the conversation.

"Maybe you're just taking your sweet-ass time," Sphinx said. "Treating yourself to all the sweet pussy Portland strip joints offer."

Her voice was too deep in its warm monotone to originate from anywhere else but an African American lineage. The tone sounded militaristic. Maybe a soldier who'd pulled multiple tours of duty in Iraq.

"Listen hard," I said. "You set up this case over the phone because it's more convenient for Stacie Burke and your schedules. You also provided sufficient proof to me that her ex-husband has never paid a cent of child support and that pursuing help through the state and civil law attorneys has reached an impasse . . ."

"What's your damage?" Sphinx said. "Do the job."

"Shut up. Let me finish. I'm getting the impression that this job isn't totally aboveboard. You girls are taking expensive precautions for a simple skip trace."

"I think you're being paranoid," Star said.

In the background of her call, I heard a hand bell resound with a ding and a speedy voice call out, *'Order of steak bites up!'*

Steak bites are a famous, mouth-watering entree at Raw Assets, a mainstream gentleman's club and steakhouse on McLoughlin Boulevard between Portland and Milwaukie.

"Then why haven't one of you met me in person since I'm working on your turf," I said, "instead of using burner phones? It shows a total lack of trust and *subterfuge* on your part."

"How did you find out that we're using burner phones?" Star blurted.

"Just now," I said in a smug tone of voice. "Ain't admission a bitch?"

"He's going to drop the case," Star said, her voice a little shaky.

"Don't lose your nerve, girlfriend," Sphinx remarked coolly. "We paid the man money. We own his smug ass."

"Yeah," I said, "you paid Alternative Investigations for a full week's worth of time, plus expenses. Very generous, ladies. But my loyalty isn't for sale here, neither is my partner's. We could just as easily refund your money. Where is Ophelia right now? I want to hear her side."

"*White boy*, please," Sphinx said. "Look at where you've been workin'. *Anyone* and *everything* can be bought at the right price. Money or not, you're gonna find Alec Winter, even if it means all you get are comp blow jobs."

Since Pepper, I found it annoying and repulsive whenever women dangled sexual favors at my base instincts like a carrot.

"You can't buy me that way," I told them, the grip on my handset tightening. "I've got my own reasons for sticking with your case. So I'll locate Stacie's ex. Then I'm going to corner all you bitches and we're going to have a goddamn heart-to-heart about what kind of trouble you're really in."

Thumbing the End button down hard to terminate the call, I shoved the cell phone inside my coat. The rain started again. Nothing but a harmless mist trying to cool my temper or dampen my spirit. I got back into the Saturn and shook the moisture out of my hair like a moody guard dog that didn't like being left outside in the cold. Drying my glasses off, I tucked them away.

I wondered what'd happened to the third woman, Ophelia.

During the phone interview, she'd done most of the talking for her friends. She spoke with a lisp. It could've been from a childhood speech impediment, learning English as a second language, or a stud left by a recent tongue piercing. I picked up on a degree of nervousness in her tone, but a lot of people struggle with that when they confide their troubles to a P.I. Her uninhibited compassion for a good friend struck emotional chords, pleading Leslie and me to take the case. We believed her conviction, and of course, the cash advance.

Cruising on up Powell, I spotted the Mustang still keeping tabs on me. The hot blonde was putting her best effort forward to negate detection. She stayed three (sometimes four) vehicles behind me and kept alternating lanes. I cracked the window for air.

Rubber squealed on slick, oily pavement and a smooth engine with perfect timing roared. I flinched and checked my mirrors. She'd powered up the horses to swerve around a dumb ass that cut her off pulling out into traffic.

Across the street from a Burger King on Fifty-First Avenue, I pulled into the Dv8 Gentleman's Club; exotic dancers and a sports bar enclosed in a purple concrete eyesore. Their billboard advertised *Gluten-Free Lap Dances*. The entrance in the back was adorned with an illustration of a provocative pin-up girl. Her smooth curves hinted at the pleasures waiting inside.

I killed a couple hours playing billiards with a stripper in chaps and a vest over a push up bra. A scream of joy made me slice a shot at the eight ball of our fourth game.

"Son. Of. A. Bitch," I shouted.

I scouted around for the source of the interruption. The hot blonde was treating herself to a table dance and slipping bills into a g-string.

My lengthy opponent bumped me aside with her hip. Slowly, she bent forward across the table. Her cleavage hovered over the felt lining. A pair of bystanders waiting for their chance to play with her gaped.

"This is for my psyche book next semester," she said with her Irish lilt.

The stripper called a corner pocket on the opposite end of the table. Her glossy bob and short bangs didn't get in the way of lining up the shot. She struck the cue ball. In geometrical arcs that would've made Einstein salivate, the eight ball bounced off each side of the table. It sunk into the corner pocket.

Setting the pool stick down gently on the edge of the table, my shoulders slumped just a little at the soreness of defeat. I surrendered a pair of Andrew Jacksons to the stripper's fingers, her long, square-tipped nails painted a glittery, clover green. She slipped the bills into her vest pocket.

"I told you a lap dance would've been cheaper," she said, running her index fingertip down my left pec and teasing my nipple.

"But not as stimulating." I winked.

She puckered her unnaturally swollen lips to blow me a kiss so long.

Heading for the door, I heard the stripper say, "Alright, lads. Which one of you wants to try and break my rack next?"

"Me! Me! I do, I do! Right here! Me!" several guys spoke up all at once.

I returned downtown a few minutes past eleven.

After parking the Saturn in the parking garage designated for the Kress Building, I hoofed it over to Ankeny and Third Avenue. I walked east on Ankeny. I stepped between a dumpster, rows of recycle bins, stacks of broken pallets, and picnic tables. Between Voodoo Donut and the Shanghai Tunnels Bar on Second Avenue, I passed a set of double glass doors in rustic wood frames covered by a half moon-shaped awning. Above the entrance a glimmering neon sign flashed: *ARDOR*. Next to that, the outline of a dancer filled up with twinkling lights. The billboard above the sign boasted *Stumptown's Burlesque Revue*.

Flanking both sides of the entrance, bouncers checked IDs, while a cashier provocatively-dressed in a pants suit at the register collected entry fees. I moved on down the double line of people huddled on the sidewalk to stand in the rear to Second Avenue. At least the rain had ceased.

I got my phone out and turned it back on. My clients hadn't left a message. Time crawled by while I stood there, my back leaned up against the brick wall.

I played a few hands of solitaire and some Tetris. A chorus of wolf whistles made me lose the game. Peeking up, I followed a pair of athletic legs up to a well-rounded ass sashaying past the line. The skin-tight green and yellow colors were unmistakable.

Within seconds, the bouncers unhooked and dropped the velvet rope.

The hot blonde breezed inside, oblivious to the booing and complaints pitched from the geeks, losers, and less-desirable waiting for their admittance.

I made it to the front of the line. When a bouncer moved a metal detector wand over my limbs and torso, of course my nipple rings caused the unit to bleep. I spread my arms and legs apart for a frisk. The bouncer efficiently and thoroughly patted me down and didn't find a concealed weapon. I rarely pack one. I don't like them.

The cashier collected the twenty-dollar cover. After handing back my ID and keys, she passed me through into an underground sprawl of stages, tables, a full-sized bar, and a kitchen setup. Strobe lights and disco balls highlighted the tanned curves of dancers hip-grinding to industrial techno beats from the Yeah, Yeah, Yeahs or Bjork. In a dark corner away from the main attractions, I found a vacant table where shadows offered some obscurity. I climbed a stool and waved to flag a waitress down.

A woman stepped out of the crowd and sidled up close.

Her thighs, wrapped up in a purple and silver pin-striped sarong, pressed gently up against mine. A flowery violet bikini top hugged her tiny breasts. Black and gray birds tattooed on her muscular upper arms fluttered their wings. A halved apple adorned her left shoulder. Sandy blonde, shoulder-length dreadlocks framed her oval face. The ends were dyed in shades of blue. Large eyeglasses amplified her bedroom brown eyes.

"Hi there, handsome. My name's Harmony. I'm a pole dancer here and at other gentleman clubs around Portland. Maybe you've seen me perform." She offered a tablet and a stylus. "This is a petition to encourage the Olympic Committee to recognize pole dancing as a sporting event. Would you please sign it?"

"Of course," I said, scribbling my signature and address without hesitation.

Catcalls exploded. I looked up from the signatures as the headliner stepped up onto the center stage. Harmony's lips curved into an admiring grin. She raised her thin and long eyebrows.

"Enjoy the show," she said, then clomped away on transparent platform heels.

The ebony beauty had on boots, a trench coat synched tightly around her waist, and a gray fedora with a black headband. Eyeliner gave her gaze, peeking out from below the slanted down snap-brim, exotic appeal. The arrogant contempt in her expression brewed black lust in the crowd for her thirty-six/twenty-three/thirty-five contours. On the wall behind the stage a silhouetted backdrop of downtown Portland, circa nineteen-forties, materialized.

"Ladies and gentlemen!" the deejay announced from his podium near the stages and kitchen pickup window. The top of his station contained amplification gear, a seventeen-inch MacBook Pro, a white iPad, and a turntable. "Ardor is proud to present the mistress of mayhem, the lady of lustful desires she demands you express. I. GIVE. YOU. Cori Bondage!"

He queued Bobby Darin's *Mack the Knife*, which ignited the stripper's slow fuse into a go-go dance and sizzling striptease. She began with prancing around and stomping her feet. Her knees and thighs jutted through the opening of the coat, alternating to the beat. She untied the belt and twirled it around before shrugging the coat off her broad shoulders to throw it out over the heads of the moshing crowd.

With a wink, she wiggled her hips and took off dangly emerald green earrings to stow them down the front of her blouse, adjusting her breasts with a 'come and get them' leer. A stripper taking off her jewelry means business.

She removed her hat to fling it. Reaching behind her head, she removed a clip, dropped it, then whipped her head down to unfurl her bouncy strips of curly hair.

From a perch on top of a circular platform that had risen out of the stage she shimmied, and pealed off a tight leopard-print blouse one button at a time. She stooped to hike up an ankle-length wool skirt for a tantalizing reveal of red silk stockings that contrasted with her dark chocolaty skin. Unzipping the back, she pushed the skirt down and stepped out of it. She kicked her suede knee-high platform boots with the rhythm. For a counterpoint she ran her hands from the naked skin of her thighs, around the curves and hollows of her abdomen, then alongside her breasts before raising both arms up to the orchestral finale of blaring horns.

As Peggy Lee's *Big Spender* boomed, her lithe carriage stretched into a yoga pose, before arching up against one of the two poles in the center of the stage. She wrapped her long, graceful legs around the top of the pole from a standing flip, and tipping upside down, wriggled out of her gold camisole to snap the stretchy fabric at outstretched hands. In anticipation of the big reveal, the audience began to chant along with the lyrics, basking in the electricity that sparked off the glow of her naked skin. Pulling herself upright, Cori hooked a leg around the smooth surface and twirled down.

She released a hidden compartment, and uncoiled a visual aid that made the crowd gasp.

Cracking the bullwhip, she pranced and preened to Nancy Sinatra's *These Boots Are Made For Walkin'*, and at the end of each verse, lashed the tip out over her audience, the dominant thwacks shocking a few patrons enough to duck or spill their drinks.

Session wrapped, Cori pulled on a cotton robe, and headed for the bar.

A bartender set a bottle of water by her long-fingered hands, and as she squeezed the refreshment between her lips, Cori's eyes fixed on mine.

Cori was really my step sister, Natty—one of a few exotic dancers reviving the art of burlesque, with whom I'd spent most of my orphan adolescence. As children, I fondly remembered the foster home where we met and the intricate jungle gym in the backyard where I watched Natty practice her acrobatics.

For my eighth birthday, she gave me my first kiss on a swing set.

I texted Natty: *Can we talk? Need your help for a case. It's important.*

She fished her handset out of her robe pocket. Reading my message, Natty's poker face revealed no emotions whatsoever. The immediate reply she sent could've gone either way.

Give me fifteen minutes to get dressed, then come on back to my office. I'll clear a path with security.

I watched Natty walk over to one of her bouncers between my table and the main entrance. His post and opposing height maintained an eagle-eyed vigil of the stages and the deejay's sound station. They traded smiles. Natty nodded my way and patted the bouncer's forearm.

He glanced at me, then his mouth articulated, "You got it."

Natty dodged and smiled at patrons, making her way over to a hallway marked *Private* on the other side of the main floor.

Fifteen minutes didn't turn into too long of a wait.

The most relaxed atmosphere I'd delved in over the last couple days emanated from Natty's place. The dancers socialized with patrons by exhibiting genuine courtesy and interest; not just their nudity.

The deejay played a wider range of music, which

the strippers certainly seemed to appreciate. Rather than just sitting or standing still in his booth, he bopped around and twirled with the beat. He reminded patrons about the house rules. He encouraged tipping with every performance. The girls dropped a few of those extra bills in his old coffee can. He smiled graciously. It was a masterful display of rhythm and timing at how he manipulated the equalizer controls or scratched vinyl.

The bouncer that Natty informed about my VIP status watched the strippers compensating the deejay with suspicion.

I stood up from the table and wove through the crowd. The joint was packing in good numbers for a Tuesday night; more women than the other places I'd been to. I supposed they enjoyed hanging out in a secure environment where men were more engrossed in the strippers than trying to pick them up. And if some guy started to harass them, then they could surely rely on one of the bouncers intervening.

I entered the long hallway. The walls were papered with a blue and silver brocade pattern.

I moved further down the hall. The music volume thumping back in the main room faded away; enough for me to recognize my own pulse again. Out of boredom and fatigue, I dragged my feet as I passed the dressing room.

Interspersed between locker doors slamming shut, I overheard exuberant chatter and laughter about clothes, makeup, and yoga. A few paces over to the left brought me to Natty's unmarked office door. I rapped with tired knuckles.

The whirring sound in the ceiling crawlspace assured me I was being scrutinized via a hidden camera. Then the electronic lock clicked. "Get in here, Matt. I don't have all night."

I opened the door, hustled inside, and shut it behind me.

Incense overwhelmed my nostrils. It failed to mask the marijuana that Natty permitted her dancers to smoke between sets. Framed photographs of her posing with movie stars that'd filmed movies in Portland over the last couple of decades, musicians, and other burlesque revivalists decorated the wall behind her. Diplomas from dance schools topped the proud display.

She had dressed down in an orange sports bra and black sweat pants, an Oregon State Beaver tried and true. Bare feet propped up on her humongous mahogany desk, she aimed a remote at the flatscreen monitor mounted on the wall near the door. Light classical music flowing from the surround system speakers stopped.

Taking her feet off the desk, Natty sprung up out of her reclined chair, then strode up to me. She wrapped her arms gracefully around my neck to hug me tight. I squeezed her hips in return and pecked her on the cheek.

"Thanks for seeing me on short notice, Natty. I know it's been a while."

"Ooo," she cooed. "You've never kissed me with

this much scruff before. Sexy."

I stepped away to take a seat in one of the leather easy chairs that faced her desk. The surface texture of the desk mimicked the grooves of an ancient Greek sculpture. It matched her persona. Natty oversaw her ventures like a goddess on a throne looking after her empire.

"Wait a minute," Natty said, hooking her fingers through one of my belt loops to pull me around. "You've gotta' see this!"

She pointed me towards the flatscreen TV. Letting me go, she skipped back behind her desk. The image of a vertical dance pole under safety mats in a gymnasium was paused on the high-res screen. I heard the metallic squeak behind me of Natty leaning back in her swivel chair to get comfy. The lights dimmed, then the picture came to life.

The strings of Bach's *Air* swirling about the office echoed like a concert in an auditorium. Harmony, the girl who'd asked me to sign the petition, walked into view. She wore a getup similar to what I saw earlier; all white silk chiffon this time. Walking ninety-degrees around the pole, Harmony sprung upward and flipped upside down. She gripped the top of the pole with her ankles and the backs of her knees. In a gentle ballet arc, she fanned both of her arms up and placed her wrists behind her back.

The classical music faded out to blast into Bjork's *Army Of Me*. Spinning down by her ankles and holding onto the hollow steel with one hand, the bracelet on her other wrist clipped a hidden clasp in the sarong. The silk unfurled. Her sheer, long legs wriggled free of the confining wrap. Harmony shimmied back up with her calves and thighs, spiraling the light fabric around her graceful curves and thick strands of dreads. Neither touched the floor.

My gaze widened and my jaw was hanging. I didn't see poetry in motion every day. The image faded out.

"Well, Matt, what do you think?"

I turned my head toward Natty in profile. "She's great. Really . . ."

Natty laughed and snorted. "You don't need to be so modest."

I winced and faced her desk. Natty's beaming expression drooped with disappointment. There was no denying that the pole dancer struck me as a beautiful thing, but my hormones weren't aroused one bit. Perspiration was dripping down my forehead and temples.

Finishing off my glass of soda, I wiggled my shirt collar. "It's hot in here, Natty. Mind if I turn the thermostat down?"

"Sure," she said, "go right on ahead."

As I moved over to the round apparatus mounted on the side wall, I felt her eyes scrutinize me with that protective concern bonded siblings share. I placed my finger on the slider control. Then I saw that the temperature was already set at sixty-nine degrees.

"This can't be right," I said, snatching a napkin from a stack on top of a mini-fridge underneath the thermostat. I wiped off my face and the back of my neck. "I'm burning up."

"There's nothing wrong with the HVAC, Matt. If my protege's natural assets aren't boosting your sex drive and your body heat is making you feel like you're trudging through a desert, maybe you should see your doctor."

I glowered at her.

"There's bottled water and soda in there," Natty said. "Help yourself."

"Thanks," I said, then opened the fridge door. I selected a tall blue and gold can that boasted sustained energy and vitamin-c.

"Bring me a lemon lime, will you?"

I popped my can open and guzzled. The sweet liquid cooled my throat and stomach. Grabbing Natty's drink, I nudged the door closed with my foot, then made my way over to the front of her desk. I set the drinks down on ceramic coasters. In lieu of breaking one of her nails opening the can, Natty grabbed a steel letter opener out of a desk drawer.

I popped the top for her. I sank down into the plush easy chair on the left of the desk. I took a deep breath, held it, then exhaled.

"That bad, huh," Natty said. "You're either still trying to get over Pepper, or you're on a case that's dragging you through Stumptown's underbelly of strip joints. Tell me about it."

I filled her in about the three strippers who'd hired me to track down Alec Winter. I included how they were avoiding face-to-face meetings with burn phones. Also, how one of them missed tonight's conference call.

"The leader of the group goes by Sphinx," I mentioned. "I think she's a vet."

"I don't know any strippers by that nickname. What did she sound like pissed off?" Natty asked.

"Like a Black Panther meeting."

"It could be Maxine Jolson," she told me. "Close friends call her Maxie. If she is financing your case to nail this bastard, you might be in some serious shit, Matt."

"Oh yeah," I said. "How's that?"

"Maxie pulled two tours in Iraq. Marine infantry. Don't ask me what happened to her there. I haven't the faintest clue. I do know that when she returned and tried to get a decent job, a lot of high-end retailers downtown slammed doors in her face."

"Why?" I asked.

"The hiring manager for the last position told her 'if a disgruntled customer got in your face, you might mis-read the situation and overreact violently because of your service in Afghanistan.'"

"Next," I said, "I bet the prick recommended she get a job in loss prevention."

Natty took a gulp of her soda pop and nodded. "He certainly did, before he got fired. A social media post going viral and newspaper interviews from all over the country saw to that. Within a day, retailers everywhere offered her an assistant manager position. Maxie turned them all down, though."

"Makes sense. I wouldn't work for a company that treated me like that either," I said, then I recognized Natty's smug grin. "Especially if a local entrepreneur made me a better offer."

"That's right," she said. "After following all the events online, I took Maxie out to dinner and obtained the salary Macy's contract offered, then added twenty-percent. Plus a fifteen-percent raise and a paid two-week vacation in the first year. It was the least I could do for a sister that put foot to ass for Uncle Sam."

"What does she do for you?" I asked.

Natty gave me a grin that fit somewhere between respect and sarcasm. "You's so cute, not assuming she's one of my strippers. Maxie did everything. She tended bar, balanced the books, bounced assholes out of my crib if they touched my girls without permission, and she stripped."

Picking up on the past tense, I said, "Sounds like you let her go, Natty. Why?"

It was her turn to breathe deeply and pick at the scab of a memory that obviously pained her. "There were certain aspects of this job where Maxie became a bit overzealous."

"For instance?" I prodded.

"Money. She caught one of the waitresses skimming,"

Natty said, "broke her wrist and her arm. The amount she stole paled in comparison to the medical bill I had to pay due to Maxie's excessive use of force."

"So that's it," I said. "You terminated her over a couple broken bones to eighty-six a thief. I don't think so, Natty. I mean, you had strong grounds to let Maxine go. But why would she go mental on a waitress skimming?"

She uncovered a flask buried under some mail and a stack of fliers. In the foreground rested a framed snapshot of our mothers in the late-sixties working at a go-go bar in San Diego. Unscrewing the cap, Natty poured clear liquid into her can of lemon lime soda until it topped off. She took a big gulp, then bit her lip.

"Care for a sip of this?" she said, offering the flask. "It's a very smooth vodka imported from—"

"Not while I'm working a case," I told her, a little snap in my 'don't change the subject' tone. "What else happened?"

"Just another asshole, Matt, that's all. He punched one of the girls. If Maxie would of just decked him back, kneed him in the nuts, and thrown him out, that would've been the end of it. She pulled a switchblade hidden in her boot though and . . . I can't sleep nights if I start to think about it. Maxie sliced his face up into a pulpy mess, like a kid carving up a jack o' lantern. He died from blood loss."

"Did the D.A. charge her?" I asked. "What about a lawsuit?"

"I got lucky," Natty said.

"Sure you did." I grunted.

Neither one of us believed in luck. After Natty and I were both dumped into foster existences because our mothers succumbed to heroin. We challenged fate by enduring turbulent times, and escaped our abusive environments.

Look at us now. Natty had become a stripper like our mothers (sans the drugs), with art and business degrees. And I can't seem to get away from strip joints, the odd case leading me back.

"Seriously. The guy had charges for assault and rape on his rap sheet longer than my legs." She paused, then continued, "My opinion? Maxie performed a public service. My insurance premiums skyrocketed after the incident though, so I had no choice. I had to let her go. I wrote her a great letter of commendation."

The lip biting stopped. Only this time Natty's eyes were averting mine, slightly gazing over my shoulder.

"Come on, Natty. You're not independently wealthy or persuasive enough to deter a D.A.'s ambition to stay in office. I'm figuring one helluva investigation led to an inquest. You were probably a character witness. And I'm betting something else about Maxine came out. Are you going to tell me what that was, or waste my time? You know I'll dig it up anyway."

"What do you care about Maxie's criminal past?" Natty argued. "You're looking for some asshole neglecting his family."

A priority email alert in my coat beeped.

"Hold on a sec," I said, then pulled my cell out of my pocket. Swiping and thumbing my password, I opened the flagged message. My face burned angry and a shade of red brighter than Natty's lipstick.

"Matt . . . what is it? What's wrong?"

"I just got the background check results on the friend Sphinx and the other two strippers needed me to help," I said. "Stacie Burke died at the age of two. The dumb bitches conjured a bogus ID with a duplicate birth certificate to hire me."

In the middle of a sip from her cocktail, Natty choked and a fine mist of the soda and vodka shot from her nostrils. Some of the fluid spattered my phone screen and hand. I wiped them off on my pant leg.

"You better get me Maxine's number," I told her.

"It's disconnected, Matt."

"Her address then."

"She lived in my guest room and moved out after the inquest."

"Getting back to that," I said. "Answer my question."

She finished wiping off and blowing her nose, then said, "A detective from San Francisco took the stand. He testified that on her eighteenth birthday, at a girl bar in the Valencia District, Maxie used deadly force to confront a bigot that was harassing her girlfriend. The judge gave her a choice: A twenty-year stretch in San Quentin for manslaughter, or enlistment in the Marine Corp."

"Do you remember the detective's names? Were

they public or private? Did the girlfriend have to testify too?"

"Enough with the questions, *goddammit*. No, I don't remember. Immediately following the inquest I went home and got very stoned."

"Alright, Natty. Okay . . ."

"Why don't you just walk away, then?" Natty said. "Since the clients are bogus and all."

"Over the past couple nights, I've already spent the money from their advance."

"That's a lot of pussy you've been watching," she said, flinching a smile.

"I've seen so much more than that, Natty," I said. "Besides, you're forgetting something about me."

"Oh yeah. What's that?" she said.

Urgent rapping at the door interrupted us.

She glared sideways to look at the seventeen-inch computer monitor atop a bamboo stand on the left. She pushed a button on a control pad built into the desk within easy reach from the right arm of her chair. The door lock clicked to disengage.

"Come in," Natty said, her voice cool, yet firm.

She reclined and put her feet back up, while her thick lips curved upward into a buzzed grin. The smell of a strong cologne or a body spray wafted around behind me. It reeked of cockiness. I craned my head around.

"Hey, boss," the deejay said, "sorry to crash your meeting. You'd told me that on my break you wanted to go over security options for the New Years Eve rave?"

"It's alright, Davy," Natty said. "I'm glad you're here. This is someone I want you to meet. Have a seat, take a load off."

The deejay sat down in the other chair next to me. Luckily I was sitting down, otherwise the potency of his aftershave would've knocked me down. Fighting the urge to wrinkle up my nose like I needed a breath of fresh air, I offered the younger guy a handshake.

"Matt Grudge," I said. "Nice to meet you, Davy."

To my surprise the deejay returned a solid clasp. His palm and fingers were rougher and more weathered than I imagined a sound geek's would be. He wore sunglasses. The frames appeared to be made of gold. At first meetings, I prefer to look a person in the eyes. The tinted lenses would conceal a tell if he was lying. It made me think that he had something to hide.

"David Helix or Deejay Volcano," he said, then flashed his other index finger up like a knife. "But *never, ever* call me 'Davy.' Only Natty's earned the privilege to call me that."

"Sure, David. Call me Matt."

"Okay," he said.

Formalities negotiated, we pushed back into our chairs. Davy's posture was at a ninety-degree angle. Shoulders slouched, I sank into the over-stuffed cushion and put my leg across my knee.

"Matt Grudge," Davy said. He repeated my name a couple more times, then snapped his fingers. "You're a private dick or something. Right . . ."

I couldn't tell if that was a question or a lame attempt to goad me into an outburst.

I smirked at the kid and gave him a title for my profession older than everyone's age in the room combined. "I'm a shamus."

"A what?"

"A shamus. You can Google it later." I switched my focus back to Natty. "What's this about a rave?"

"I'm hosting one on New Years Eve, and Davy here is supplying all the musical entertainment. Several of my dancers will be attending also. The night's going to rock, huh Davy?"

"Yeah, yeah. You know it! The last detail we need is a security expert capable of making sure all the fire exits are up to code, watching security monitors, backing up the bouncers, and insulating the event from any potential illegal activities. Interested, Matt?"

"Piece a' cake," I said.

"Terrific, dude. Here's me." He handed over a glossy business card.

I tilted the expensive stock. A 3D volcano under a blazing logo spewed musical notes.

"Cool," I said in a dull tone. "My number's in the book. Leave me a message with the address where the party's going to be. I'll give the building a once over and then we can talk about my fee."

We stared off at each other for a minute. If I could've seen the expression behind his expensive sunglasses I'm positive it would have been asking, 'Is that it?'

Smirking, I tucked his card away in my left shirt pocket. "Catch you later, Deejay Volcano."

The kid got up to leave. Halfway there he spun around. His agility lent itself to a martial arts discipline. The last time someone moved in my presence that fast, they were aiming a gun at me.

"I almost forgot, Natty," he said.

"What's that, Mr. Deejay?"

"There's a girl at the bar wearing a faded rose-colored sweater. She just arrived in town and she's looking for a ride out to that newer vegan joint."

"Soy Toy, world's premier vegan strip club," I said, turning my face back around at Natty. The clock on my phone read that time was nearly midnight. "My last destination for the night before all the bars close in a couple hours. I'll take her with me."

Natty rolled the mouse. I supposed she was tightening a closeup on the girl. She cocked an eyebrow. "*Damn*, bitch is drawing a lot of patrons away from the stages."

"It's her British accent," the deejay said. "Sexy as hell. She came in out of the last downpour."

"What's her name?" I asked. Davy didn't answer me. "You mean you got all that, but you didn't get her name?"

Holding up his right fist, the deejay used his other fist to turn a pretend crank, which raised up his middle finger.

"Snappy gesture," I said. "It's been around since

before you were diaper trained, kid." At least I didn't call him, 'Davy.'

"Know what," he said, "I bet there are plenty of other asshole private eyes in the book."

"Sure are," I said. "None of them will blend into your rave like I can though."

"Boys, boys," Natty called out. "Keep your dicks in your pants. David, we're hiring Matt and his partner for the job. Would you please tell London Chick that Matt will be out in a few minutes to give her a *ride*."

Davy slammed the door shut on his way out. I stood up and moved around to the back of Natty's desk. She was still staring at the girl on the crisp black and white surveillance feed.

London Chick was sitting on a stool at the bar, her silky white legs crossed.

"Natty, please do me a quick favor. Bring up a grid."

"Sure," she said, moving the pointer and clicking the mouse. "Looking for something?"

Standing shoulder to shoulder with Natty, I saw the scars across her knuckles. They were disciplinary mementos from learning how to handle a bullwhip.

I panned a hard look at all the angles. The hot blonde was jostling a *Terminator 2* pinball machine to control the ball. I tapped the screen.

"Someone," I said. "This woman has been following me all night."

Natty picked up her phone. "I know how to get her off your tail."

THREE

Matt Grudge

Stripped down to her lacy panties, the stripper crawled up onto the hot blonde's lap. *Suicide Blonde* blasted throughout the club. Disco ball lights spun about the dimmed atmosphere. The freckles on the stripper's bare skin shone like sapphires.

The stripper wriggled her torso and pushed her breasts in closer against the blonde. She bowed her head into the blonde's ear. My stalker's luscious lips opened wide to hoot a cheer. The stripper took this as a cue to grind faster. She stopped flailing her arms with the rhythm to place the blonde's hands on her thighs.

Kissing Natty goodnight, I dashed out of her office.

Once I reached the hallway entrance, I slowed down

and walked a nonchalant, direct path over to London Chick. My broad shoulders and weight training from my wrestling days came in handy. I nudged a couple guys crowding her aside. I didn't want to start a brawl. "Make a hole."

"What the . . .?"

"Dick head."

"Wait your turn."

"Jerk off."

"Fuck off."

"Hi," I said, offering London Chick my hand as if I intended to escort her to a black and white ball. "My name's Matt Grudge. I'm going to Soy Toy. Want a lift?"

Underneath her well-warn sweater, a delicate knit blouse with teensy polka dots still stuck to her damp skin in mouth-watering places around her small breasts and the sculpted hollows of her abdomen. The ends of her sandy brown hair barely reached her shoulders. She brushed long, moist bangs away from her Caribbean blue eyes to size me up and down.

"Well," she said, placing her cup of tea on the bar. "You don't look like the sort to escort a lady. Looks can be deceiving though, and so far, I approve of your initiative." Placing her fingers in my grasp, London Chick grabbed her bag and hopped off the bar stool.

Her thick British accent prickled the hairs inside my ears.

"Right this way," I said, walking us toward the front exit.

I looked to my left where the couches for lap dances lined the walls. The hot blonde caught sight of me and turned her face away from the stripper's erect, studded nipples to see me leaving. The stripper earned every penny of her distracting performance. Gently, she cupped the hot blonde's face in her hands and moved her mouth toward the blonde's.

I didn't waste another second to watch and led London Chick out into the alley. I noticed we were still holding hands. She didn't seem to mind. I double-timed it for the Kress Building parking area.

"What's the rush?" London Chick asked.

"It's going to rain again soon," I said. "I can smell it."

I opened the Saturn's passenger side door, then waved my hand to invite her to get in. Jogging around to the driver's side, I hopped in and cranked the engine on. I pulled out of the reserved lot and headed north for Burnside.

"Weird," she said, "with an exclamation point," pointing at the black and yellow mural on the back of Dante's, a nefarious goth and punk bar. "I think I'm going to like Portland."

The traffic light clicked on red. I floored the brakes. Barely-legal youths on a pub crawl swaggered drunkenly in the cross walk. She ignored them, staring at my muscular arms instead.

Natty's text alert sounded. Pam Grier said, 'You're under arrest, sugar.' I unlocked my phone to read: *Haul ass! Blonde stalker dumped dancer in another guy's lap to chase U. She's a COP. By the way, Maxie and Davy were tight.* Natty attached a YouTube link.

I'd have to check her tips out later. My eyes darted to the rear view mirror, looking out for the restored Mustang. The light turned green.

"Better tighten your seatbelt," I told London Chick as I stomped on the gas and sped west onto Burnside.

"What do you do for a living?" she asked.

"I'm a private investigator."

Top marks to London Chick for not bursting out with laughter.

"Wow! That's fascinating. You've obviously upgraded the mold from Spade or Marlowe."

I threaded the Saturn through light traffic. The rain had stopped. I sped up.

"What do you do?" I asked.

London Chick's head collapsed on the head rest. The pulse in her long, graceful neck quickened. "Amongst other things, I'm a vegan chef."

I knew she was holding something back. It wasn't any of my business.

"You're in the right town for that," I said. "Portland has a huge vegan population."

I filled her in briefly about the mini-mall on Stark, and the grocery store chains that catered more to a plant-based eating lifestyle, Whole Foods and New Seasons.

I became aware that London Chick seemed to be studying me. I actually thought about telling her a little more about myself.

For instance, the happier times I'd spent in a foster home life. Watching stoic detective movies and munching on burnt, salty popcorn by the handful with my step dad. The couch potato lifestyle led to him suffering a heart attack.

After burying her husband, my step mom couldn't afford to take care of me. I got moved back to an orphanage until my biological grandfather tracked me down and strong-armed his son into finally admitting I was his flesh and blood, and to take me in.

Coping with abandonment had made me distrust attention. And just because London Chick accepted my offer for a lift didn't entitle me to dump my depressing youth on her.

I switched the blinker on and cruised right onto the exit for the northwest industrial section. During the rest of our trip to Soy Toy, I gave her the cool and silent treatment.

"You're on a case right now," she said. "Aren't you."

"Maybe . . ."

"Tease! What are you looking for? I bet it's a cheating spouse, huh," she pressed, melting the ice.

I pulled into a steep, uphill sloped parking lot. "We're here."

After I opened the car door for London Chick, we leisurely walked towards the main side entrance. Loose gravel crunched beneath our shoes. I spotted a police cruiser camped out in the lot across the street. Rainwater had puddled in the seats of a pair of plastic deck chairs about fifteen-feet to the right of the glass door.

London Chick bumped her hip against mine. "Thanks for driving me out here, Matt. Cab fare would've cost me a bloody fortune."

On a poster in a glass frame mounted to the left of the entrance, the silhouette of a dancer in a ballet pose with soybean-shaped pasties bid us welcome. A billboard above this read *Flick the Bean Friday-Dildo & Vibrator Shows*.

"My pleasure," I said, pulling the door open and waving her inside.

We headed right down a long hallway for twenty-feet before it turned ninety-degrees left. Duran-Duran's *Hungry Like The Wolf* played up the fun atmosphere. Once we reached the archway at the end of the L-shaped passageway, we entered the main room.

Two long stages with spinning poles dominated the center. Three dancers of various shapes and sizes performed. The bar resided in the back. A drum set and a throne sat on top of the bar area. I told the topless bartender that this was my first time here and enquired what was good on the menu.

She shook her floppy tits, hands waving. "Boobs and booze, hon!"

I ordered two beers.

"Oh, I'll get those," London Chick said.

"My treat." I paid with a twenty and all of my change came back in two-dollar bills. "What's this?" I asked the bartender.

"Tip our dancers and find out, sweetie pie," she said.

As I watched the bartender shave the heads of foam off our glasses with a straight razor, I overheard London Chick ask a dancer strutting by where she could find the manager. The stripper's bulky thigh-high platform boots thudded on the hardwood floor. London Chick wanted to submit her resume and fill out an application for a cook position that she'd read about in the *Oregonian's* Classifieds section.

While she went to go chat with the manager, I took our beading pint glasses topped with lemon wedges to a booth. After squeezing the juice into the bubbling amber brew, I took a big swallow of the lager. Leaning my back against the wall, I relaxed my neck and shoulders against the seat cushion. I felt pretty good in spite of the case going to shit.

I looked to the stages and winced. The strippers here took their clothes off faster than any of the other dives I'd surveilled. An illusion of seduction didn't exist. A patron placed a pair of two-dollar bills on the ledge in front of him. The red-headed stripper caressed his beard. I found her glittering lips curved up in an enticing grin easy to read. 'Sit very still, handsome.'

Tumbling forward, the red head placed the crown of her head into the man's lap. She took his huge fingers and placed them on her waistline to help her stay balanced. Legs rising up, she split them apart to show off her genitalia mere inches from the guy's nose.

I sat through thirty-minutes more of eighties hits. Every once in a while, I peered around the room, still on the lookout for Alec Winter or the blonde cop. A dancer that'd just put her bikini back on after her set walked by a bouncer. He slyly pulled the knot on her top. She spun around and slapped him. I started to get up, then sat back down. He took the blow and shrugged. Cursing, the dancer stomped off.

I thought about watching the video Natty texted me. The joint was too loud. I did send her Alec Winter's photograph and asked her to share it with any girls she knew to be discreet enough, then to let me know if he surfaced. She replied: *Sure. Why the hell not.* I finished my beer.

I saw a patron offering a greenback to a dancer with his teeth. Throughout the night, I'd watched more money exchange hands than a bank teller processes deposits on payday. My gears started to turn. So many criminal enterprises thrived in cash-intensive environments such as this.

My light buzz churned up repressed memories. My old man was an asshole, barely acknowledged my existence. Numbers drew his attention more than my accomplishments ever could. Instead of working the streets, he preferred to chase crooks on spreadsheets. I was beginning to see a universal truth applicable to this case.

Follow the . . .

London Chick slung her purse down on the table.

She plopped down next to me. Her lips stiffened and her jaw tightened.

"Only part-time," she shouted. "The ad didn't mention that. If you call five-to-ten hours a week part time. Bullocks! Then the slimy asshole offered me a full-time stripping job. According to a sign by the dressing room entrance, girls are fined if they don't remove their gear fast enough. Bullshit."

"Can I get you something stronger to drink than beer?"

"No," she said, releasing a long, disappointed sigh.

London Chick rested her temple on my shoulder. She didn't move a muscle when the lights flickered. The deejay yelled, "First call!"

"Did the cheater ever show up?" London Chick asked, her voice weary.

"I can't talk about cases."

She waved a disapproving hand at the stage. "I'm not going to bare it all for a sweaty handful of greenbacks in my G-string. Fuck that. I've posed for art universities and publishing houses."

"You'll figure something out," I said.

London Chick lifted her head up and turned around. Her hair tangled in my whiskers.

"Let's get outta' here," she breathed in my ear, her lips brushing my earlobe. Her low-pitched voice steamed up my senses. She'd scooted around sideways on the bench for a more direct approach. I also became aware of London Chick's hand resting on my thigh, gently sliding in towards my crotch. "Shagging a P.I. is on my bucket list."

I turned my face at London Chick's sharply. "I don't even know your name."

She didn't flinch. Her shimmering eyes faced mine like a predator on the hunt. Her crooked lips were parted enough to see a glimpse of teeth, also parted slightly. Her tongue was wriggling with anticipation, primed to devour something succulent and sweet.

"Alison. Call me Ali."

"Last call!" the deejay shouted, playing with the lights again.

I leaned in and kissed her. I tasted vanilla on her lips. Her tongue explored my mouth first before I reciprocated. As our tongues entwined, Ali moaned. She wrapped her arms around me.

I felt a tap on my shoulder. "Hey you two, get a room."

His gruff monotone sounded like a bouncer's. We ignored him and kept making out.

FOUR

Leslie Crow

Sails billowing, the Seaward Symphony, a Dana 24 sailboat, cruised out of the Bay. Low-velocity and turbulent winds were blowing my long hair everywhere. The vessel's flat transom sliced through a choppy wave with a crash of white noise. I grabbed onto the railing. A mist of seawater sprayed across my face.

I screamed with a sense of fun I hadn't experienced since my first roller coaster ride.

The boat's captain and navigator, Ling Shui Li, sat across from me on the deck astern. She confidently moved the rudder back and forth across her thighs. She smirked knowingly.

"First time on a sailing yacht, Miss Crow?"

"Yes, it is. And please, call me Leslie."

"You're the detective who delivered Dee-Dee's ashes," Ling said. "That's a very honorable errand."

Daniil climbed up onto the deck through the cabin

passageway. He handed me a cup of coffee. "Everything alright? I thought I heard a scream."

I took a sip of the piping hot joe. It warmed me up and matched my all black wardrobe: a new pair of jeans, a t-shirt, a turtleneck sweater, a denim jacket, and my riding boots. "I didn't mean to alarm you. We struck a wave and I forgot why I was here for a second."

Daniil sat down next to me and put a consoling arm around my shoulders. "Leslie, I'm so happy you're here. I know Dee would be moved by your presence too. How you grieve is none of my business, but I assure you that not everything about her final journey today is sadness. She would've wanted you to have a good time in her memory."

I pecked him on the cheek and hugged his neck.

Ling maneuvered the Seaward Symphony past Alcatraz. Her steely expression of respect and wisdom for sailing glided with the ocean. Beads of water from the craft's wake covered her transparent poncho. Underneath she wore a blouse and wool skirt.

San Francisco's skyline got smaller and smaller on the horizon. About a mile out beyond the Golden Gate Bridge, Ling dropped anchor. Daniil took my cup into the galley to dispose of it for me. When he came back out he was accompanied by his life-partner Noah and a girl who'd known Dee since junior high. I couldn't remember her. It made no difference to me though, because Dee and I attended different schools.

Dee-Dee and I met in Valencia when I wandered

into an all girl bar. She was trying out a fake ID and I was on the run from a pair of police officers chasing me for shoplifting a box of condoms. It was a dumb gang initiation dare.

Noah handed Daniil a backpack, which he slung over one shoulder. The five of us traversed the side decks on the non-slip pattern molded onto the fiberglass. I was amazed by how the twenty-four-foot craft didn't roll very much. I heard gears turning. Ling was lowering and securing the sails.

The girl whose name I couldn't recall took a seat on the foredeck at the front of the cabin. She took off her heels and tucked her feet in under her rear, sitting sideways. I plopped down next to her, legs apart, arms resting on my knees. The cabin surface made a great backrest. Ling and Noah sat down just in front us.

Daniil stood at the bow. He thanked us all for being there at such short notice. Then he unzipped his backpack and pulled out a thin hardcover book with a warn out spine. He turned the volume around to show off the cover.

The Cat In The Hat.

"When I first moved to the States," Daniil began, "I spoke just enough English to get by, but reading it was a totally different concept to grasp. This was my first reader. When she was four, Dee often helped me sound out the words. The most peculiar thing though is that when Dee couldn't fall asleep at nap time or at bedtime, reading Dr. Seuss to her in my native tongue would put her out faster than a glass of warm milk. So, my friends, I think this is an appropriate moment to read Dee her favorite story, and help her rest."

Daniil read the timeless children's classic in Ukrainian.

A stiff wind tried to pull an unbound page from the book. He snatched the page between his fingertips. Once he was finished, tears streaming down his face, Daniil returned the book to his pack and withdrew the heart-shaped box.

Stepping up to the edge of the bowsprit platform, he wedged a foot against the varnished teak surface. He waited a few minutes for the wind to blow away from the bow. The weather yielded. Daniil unsealed the container and turned it over.

Dee's ashes powdered the sea. The tide carried her remains throughout the eternal fathoms.

●

I got back to the bed and breakfast a little after 12 p.m.

"Hey, Leslie," one of the drag queens lounging in the living room and painting his nails called out. "Can I help glam you up, girlfriend?"

My fingernails were in sad shape, last month's polish flaking off. He'd probably noticed them last night while we played poker for matchsticks with his friends into the wee hours.

"I'll take a raincheck, Jeff," I said, muffling a yawn with my hand. "I need to get some rest."

The surveillance job started tonight. I'd already reacquainted myself with public transit routes yesterday. The release of emotions at Dee's funeral had left me somewhat drained. After closing the drapes on a dreary, overcast Wednesday, I stripped, then stretched out on the Queen-sized bed. I set the alarm on my iPhone for thirty-minutes.

I slept through it.

I tossed and turned, my unquenched thirst for vengeance tangling up the sheets. Yeah, I realized that to a degree Pepper was a victim too. Be that as it may, I yearned to strangle the heartless, conniving slut until her tongue protruded through her lips and turned blue. I awakened from a nightmare, my chest heaving to breathe.

The power nap turned into two hours.

A lukewarm shower washed away the sweat and the fragmented details from my bad dream. I pulled on a pair of stone-washed jeans slashed in all the right places for my comfort and ventilation. I completed my wardrobe: a white T-shirt with a faded Portland garage band logo over my black bra, a beige flannel button down, green fleece jacket, and of course, my riding boots. I also took my Nikon.

I had just enough time to check one last thing off my fun list before my vacation officially ended. Stowing the camera in one of the pods on my bike, I motored up to the north end of the city. I stole a glimpse of the Presidio and smelled the diesel from pleasure craft in the marina.

The traffic was starting to thicken with camper trailers, RVs, and a VW van covered in peace sign decals and a pot leaf painted on the back. My memory flashed on one of my mom's hitchhiking stories from the sixties. At that time, she found that hippie stoners were the most hospitable of the white man. They had the best snacks, too.

I pulled into the parking area near the Roundhouse gift shop, a stone's throw away from the Golden Gate Bridge.

Huddling and squeezing around other tourists, I picked out a few souvenirs. I stuck to smaller items or things I could wear. I got a tall shot glass for Matt. I fingered through a bin of watercolor paintings and regretted that I didn't have the space on my bike to get one. Kids not watching where they were going tripped me up a couple times. The same clerk asked me if I needed help three times with keen eye contact and a pasted-on smile. I supposed that in my dingy threads I kinda looked like a potential shoplifter.

I trotted down the steps to my bike, then froze.

A silver Lincoln with tinted windows was blocking my Streetfighter in along with at least two other cars. Exhaust trailed from the luxury vehicle's tailpipe. The last time I saw a silver Lincoln, practically identical to this one, it was illegally parked at a crime scene on Squaw Mountain in Estacada.

The back door clicked and swung open. A stocky man with a high-and-tight buzz cut stepped out. He wore Armani. His suit coat bulged under his armpit. Sunglasses masked a set of eyes undoubtedly scanning the people milling around for threats.

Another fellow crawled out of the back seat. He supported his stout frame and generously-sized potbelly with a cane. I'd seen stock video of him on international news and heard his name dropped during my investigation into Dee's murder.

"You know who I am, Miss Crow," he said.

"Ambassador Sacha Ivanovich." I nodded. "What brings you out here on a dismal afternoon? I'm sure there are better mementos and historical icons at the Russian embassy."

"Da," he said, chuckling. "I mean yes, there are. I was wondering if you would do an old man the pleasure of walking with him halfway out on the bridge. My doctor tells me this helps to keep my cholesterol down."

"Join a gym," I said.

The bodyguard frowned and took his hand off the car door. I wondered how fast I'd be able to drop my bag of goodies and pull my knife before the angered Russian bear tried to wrestle me into the Lincoln.

"Halt, Peter," the ambassador said. Peter stopped. "Miss Crow is quite right. Enough beating around the bush and wasting her time. I need to talk to you about a case, detective—a case I believe you're already vested in."

"Wouldn't a meeting like this be more appropriate in your office, or at your home, Ambassador?"

"Those places have ears I can't afford to have overhear what I want to hire you for," Ivanovich said. "Besides, these tourists are too occupied with the spectacles and romance of San Francisco to pay us any attention."

A Russian diplomat and an American Indian out for a stroll on one of the world's renowned landmarks, I thought. *Sure, nobody's going to notice that.*

"Can I put my stuff away?" I asked.

The ambassador raised a hand and snapped his fingers. Another bodyguard I never saw coming appeared out of the crowd beside me. He slowly reached for the handle of my bag and toted my souvenirs over to the Lincoln.

Ivanovich and I made for the ramp that lead to the double-wide sidewalk. The tip of his cane clacked against the concrete walkway. The ambassador hobbled, his knees making an occasional crackling sound. His knuckles, especially the ones wrapped around the support aid, were more pronounced. Arthritis is a bitch.

I slowed down for him. The Golden Gate loomed overhead before us. The suspension bridge's sulfur color stood out, even with the gloomy patches of fog that were hovering near.

"So, here we are," Ivanovich said, "on a structure built by an engineer whose peers argued would be too expensive, a monstrosity, and distracting. In a word: Impossible. Did you know that 600,000 rivets were driven into the two towers?"

"One of my great uncles worked on the construction site. America's first hard hat area," I told him. "Listen, Ambassador, remember what you said back there about not wasting my time. Skip the history lesson."

"This bridge connects a great amount of tourism and commerce to this city. I bet you just spent a small fortune back at the gift shop, and this route takes a lot of San Franciscans to their homes or jobs in outlying counties. This is a kind of truth, isn't it." I nodded, mostly to keep him talking, but I got the picture. "You're going to be my bridge to the truth I'm seeking in Portland, Miss Crow."

Oh, terrific. Metaphors now. "I don't understand."

"Recently, I journeyed to the Rose City in hopes of convincing the lawmakers there to open a joint-probe into human trafficking that's existed there since the late eighteen hundreds. All they did was give me a red carpet tour of the city and hold an expensive gala-style dinner in my honor. The caviar was horrid. Don't get me started on the vodka. They used tourism and commerce to evade my concerns."

"Anticipating this kind of subterfuge to my request," he continued, "I pulled some strings and contacted a pair of former Spetsnaz operatives that retired to Seattle. They preceded my arrival and gathered much intelligence for me. One of them disappeared while staking out a farmhouse in Damascus, the other was seriously wounded in a burned out church, and most likely would've perished, if it weren't for a local private detective stumbling on the same clues he'd followed."

"Cut to the chase, Ambassador."

"Fair enough," he said. "One of the Jane Does found in that fire was my niece, Ursula. I brought her to San Francisco to pursue a Journalism major. I don't know how, but she came across a human trafficking pipeline. She believed it starts in Southeast Asia, reaches across the Pacific to San Francisco, then drops down into Brazil. You'll read all about it. Before my operatives arrived in Portland, I received a package from Ursula. She must've been in terrible danger at the time. Her beautiful calligraphy was scribbled on the envelope. I traced the postmark to a mailbox on Southeast Twenty-Second Street, near an entrance to the Brooklyn Rail Yard."

"What was in the package?" I asked.

"The journal I gave to Ursula on her eighteenth birthday when she decided to pursue investigative journalism. Peter is depositing it in your bag of mementos now. Using Ursula's notes, I want you to find the savages who killed my niece. Any. Means. Necessary."

Almost halfway out over the strait, a frigid breeze across the length of the bridge. I caught a chill and zipped up my jacket.

"This sort of investigation will cost a lot of money," I said, my teeth chattering and my body shivering.

"I've already enclosed a cash advance in the journal. I think you will find it exceptionally generous."

"What about signing a contract for my services?"

"There can be no paper trail for this case, Miss Crow. And I'm not worried about signatures binding our business. I know you're committed to this case I'm offering for personal reasons. As a matter of fact, if you should complete this case before the year is up, I'll throw in a bonus."

"What's that exactly?" I said.

"By that time, I will know the precise whereabouts of Pepper Rourke. I'll tell you where to find her."

My hands clenched into fists. Good thing I didn't get that manicure. The pressure would've drawn blood. I took a deep breath and relaxed my hands.

"After I find the persons responsible," I said, "what happens next?"

"There's a burn phone in the bag. Text the coordinates once you've got a location and can guarantee they'll be occupied for thirty-minutes. My people will mobilize in fifteen. In return, Pepper Rourke's whereabouts will be transmitted. The fate of the criminals you find doesn't need to keep you up nights."

I envisioned blood-stained medical instruments and greasy engine tools laid out on a metal table in a scrap yard garage.

"Maybe we should involve the law at that point," I said.

"It's your choice, Miss Crow. I understand a woman in your position has a certain ethical code to uphold. Just so you know, that decision would nullify the Pepper bonus."

"Okay, Ambassador, I'll take the case."

"Thank you, Leslie." Winded, he stopped. "Well, this as far as I can go. Peter will put your bag in the storage compartment on your bike. Don't worry, he won't leave any scratches picking the lock."

"Ambassador, hold it, please. I have just one more question."

Ivanovich took a deep breath and looked up at me. "Yes?"

"Did you have any of your men try to follow me, size me up for the job? Possibly an albino wearing his hair in a ponytail."

"I demand my people maintain a strict dress code and keep themselves well-groomed. No man on my staff would ever wear a . . . ponytail."

Ambassador Ivanovich finished turning around to go back.

Moseying up to the rail, I took in the panoramic view. The angles and far reach of the human trafficking underworld I'd been hired to infiltrate and expose filled me with dread. The majesty of the Bay couldn't distract me from the souls consumed by a dark industry.

●

The surveillance job started out easy. The client's son was a bookworm. He met up with his three friends, another guy and two young women on the northwest corner of the main library, marked with a giant revolving "L" sculpture, in the Civic Center at 5 p.m.

While pretending to shoot other historic landmarks

around the scenic area, I swiveled around to sneak profile shots of the couples. Good thing I wasn't taking pictures to sell to a newspaper or a magazine. The overcast atmosphere made the image quality too dreary to be commercial.

Gavin Steinberg, son of Oregon Republican Senator Ruth Steinberg, was devouring a hardback novel. One leg crossed over the other, he was sitting on top of the short retaining wall that bordered the library. The hardback novel rested on his raised knee. The title read *Nightmare Town*. His thin-browed, deep-set eyes scanned rapidly. Licking his fingers, he turned pages.

A tall brunette, her coarse hair, just an inch past shoulder length that curved off in a gentle wave, plopped down next to my client's boy. Her cheeky buttocks cushioned the landing. A gray wool overcoat, unbuttoned, flaunted her high, well-rounded breasts in a tight, purple cashmere sweater. Stretching her long, blue jean-clad gymnast legs out over the concrete pathway, she crossed her sky-high, platform-heeled boots. The silver hoops in her septum and nostrils glinted in the pink, golden sunset. She nuzzled up against Steinberg to rest her head on his shoulder.

Her full red lips puckered and she said something that I was too far away to decipher. Steinberg ignored her. She held her hand up, palm out, at an even level next to the book. The gold engagement ring that boasted a teardrop-cut diamond sparkled. Walking parallel to the couple, I snapped a shot of the rock. She kissed him firmly on the cheek. The book geek surrendered enough of his concentration to smile wanly. The brunette had to wipe her lipstick off Steinberg's milky-white skin. I wondered if Steinberg had ever sounded out sunlight.

His guy friend saw the brunette's show of affection. His crooked mouth, scowling with anger, made his square jaw jut out.

Jealous much?

At about a quarter past the hour, a stocky fellow wearing tan slacks, a white dress shirt, a tie, a beige trench coat, and a brown fedora walked up to Steinberg, his companions, and myself. I liked his no nonsense gait. He had a schedule to keep. A strong breeze snatched his tie; the fabric waved. I could make out the design of a falcon on the fabric.

"My apologies for being late," he said, "but I had to take a detour around some intoxicated transients fighting over a knife. With that said, the tour skirts the Tenderloin. So please, stay together, and the next two-to-three hours should go by without incident."

A few more people showed up: two mystery writers, one "Bogie" fan. I didn't know what that meant. I stifled a yawn when the tour guide gave me a friendly hello and asked if I intended to join the group. I said sure and paid the bearded man.

"What brings you to San Francisco?" he asked.

"Oh . . . I'm shooting an art book about the architecture and the history of the Bay Area," I said, looking him clear in the eye.

"That sounds original," Steinberg's fiancé snickered.

The snide remark slid down my back.

Giving the entire group an inviting smile, I said, "Hey! How about a group picture free of charge? I'll e-mail or text it to you." I looked at the guide. "That is, if we have enough time."

"Sure," he said. "Just make it quick."

Everyone cheered at the gesture.

Over the next two hours the guide narrated a detailed history about Dashiell Hammett, a white novelist that elevated mystery novels into literature. His work as a Pinkerton detective had given his narrative style an authenticity other writers of the day had lacked.

My mom told me a story about the Pinkerton detectives once.

A pair of them came to the res in the fifties to arrest my great uncle who'd been a getaway driver for a bank robbery. They'd probably been hired by the bank after the government had already made up the loss, in order to get back the money for a reasonable "finder's fee," say, 20-percent of what they found. Once they'd secured him with irons, they had to transport him off the res, but their coupe didn't have enough room in the backseat.

Instead the ruthless thugs lashed my great uncle to the top of their car like a slaughtered elk.

We walked a loop near the edge of the Tenderloin, crested Nob Hill, then precipitated toward Union Square and a finish at John's Grill, a legendary chop house. The guide recommended the rack of lamb.

My client's son declined.

"We have other engagements," his fiancé said.

"Things to do. Other places to explore," their companions added.

Frankly, I was glad that the tour was over. The fiancé *popped* wads of strawberry bubblegum with relish. I wanted to rap her right in the mouth.

Hanging back far enough, I acted as if I intended to go my own way also. I tossed a few dollars into a street performer's open guitar case. She wore a tarnished copper butterfly clip in her ash blonde hair. She crooned an acoustic cover of *Losing My Religion* in an operatic soprano voice.

I crossed the bustling street.

Unslinging my go-bag, I set it down on top of a newspaper box. I stored my digital camera in the main compartment. I peeled the sleeves of my unbuttoned flannel shirt off. Sweat was beginning to ooze through my pores. The Bikini Kill T-shirt I had on underneath would be warm enough. Stuffing the flannel around the camera for insulation, I removed one more clothing accessory before zipping the bag closed. A plain baseball cap.

I squinted up the avenue to reacquire my subjects. Slinging my go-bag back over my shoulder, I double-timed it to catch up.

Steinberg's fiancé whistled to hail a cab.

"Damn it . . . "

I huffed it up the slight upgrade, bobbing and

weaving around other pedestrians. I saw the four of them squeeze into a black and white taxi. I reached the intersection. I really needed to cross it, or I'd lose them. The pedestrian signal red hand was flashing and counting down at 5 seconds.

Fuck it! I darted out into the street like a rabbit trying to outrun a hawk.

Ten feet from the opposite corner, a gold Ferrari turning right cut me off. I hurdled sideways over the hood. My ass and hip made a dent. Touching down on the flat heels of my riding boots, I heard his curses and his horn blaring.

A hack stumbled out of a smoke shop half-a-block up. He stepped into his yellow taxi. The light on top switched to *On Duty*.

I wrenched the back door open and hopped inside. The seat cushions were lumpy and reeked of nicotine and fast food grease.

"Follow that cab," I panted, pointing, "and I'll pay double what's on the meter."

He whipped out into traffic before I could even shut the door.

FIVE

Leslie Crow

Dragging my boot heels, I trudged up the steep steps of the bed and breakfast. I clasped the decorated oval knob. The smooth brass was cold to touch. A frosty dew rubbed off on my skin. Puffs of my breathing evaporated in the stark hue of the porch light. I wanted a bath, a cup of coffee, and a thick afghan to wrap my exhausted body up in.

I opened the red door and entered the parlor. The lights in the lounge to my left were off. I could just see the outlines of the antique, restored wing chairs, the love seat, the armoire carved out of figured maple that housed a flatscreen TV, and the five-tier bookshelf. The top shelves held leather-bound books. DVDs and board games were stored on the middle and bottom shelves.

A pair of gold, exotic eyes on top of one of the chairs flared at me. Startled for a second, I stared right back at them. It was just the owner's house cat, a Bombay named Bart. After regarding me indifferently, he went back to licking his paws and rubbing his face.

To my right, a banker's lamp illuminated the bar, which doubled as a check-in desk. The twenty-something college student sitting on a stool behind the wooden counter had her nose buried in a textbook. Her brown eyes, which were almost too big for her eyeglasses, looked up at me briefly.

"Hi," she said, giving me a wry smirk. "Can I help you with anything?"

I muttered no.

The college student looked back down at her studies. Her strands of ash blonde hair dangled over a tablet she was tapping on with a stylus. I could make out the calculous equations reflected in her glasses.

I began to step toward the staircase straight ahead. I heard a rolling purr and came to a halt before I stepped on something. Bart's long body was curling around my heels.

"That's a first," the student said.

"What's that?" I asked.

"Bart usually ignores strangers. I've been jockeying this desk for over a year now and he won't even talk to me when I open up a can of his food. Stuck-up little scavenger."

Bart continued to rub his well-groomed fur up against my riding boots. He cocked his head toward the sound of the student's voice. He meowed in an aggressive tone.

It sounded like *fuck you* in feline.

I looked down at the wriggling fur ball. "Where's your old man?"

Bart purred louder.

"He drove the resident drag queens to an Indian casino gig up north," the student said. "They won't be back for a couple days."

I stepped around the cat and moved into the kitchen behind the check-in desk. The lights were off, but the ambience from the banker's lamp shined enough for me to find my way. I skirted the dining room table where I'd played cards with the drag queens the other night. Opening a cupboard, I grabbed a small ceramic bowl and a saucer.

I headed upstairs. Before the steps began to spiral, I paused and turned in profile. I looked to see if Bart was still lingering by the bar. He was watching me.

"Well, come on," I said, waving at the cat and patting my thigh. "You can hang out with me."

After reaching the second floor, I didn't wait for him and kept walking with a fatigued gate for my room. I removed the bronze skeleton key from my front pocket. I inserted it in its hole and turned the heart-shaped bow.

I opened the door and a patter of paws scurried down the hall. Uttering a quick meow, Bart darted inside my room.

"Took you long enough," I said, smirking at his whirling tail.

I followed him in and locked the door. It dawned

on me how the little critter could get out to use his litter box. Then I spotted the outline of a kitty door in one of the lower panels. Stooping forward, I pulled the lever that otherwise kept it secured if guests didn't want to receive a visit from the housebroken pet.

Bart bumped my ankle and meowed curtly. He leapt up onto the bed. Housekeeping had remade it tightly with hospital corners. His delicate paw prints barely left impressions on the flannel duvet cover as he slunk up to the headboard and sniffed the pillows.

Lifting the satchel strap off my shoulders and over my head, I hung my bag from the hook on the door. I pivoted around and moved toward the bed. The reflective silence of the cozy room was putting my senses in a state of euphoria. I'd just spent the last five hours following Steinberg and his pals all over San Francisco's nightspots. The noise of loud music and raised voices in conversation still echoed in my ears.

I sat down at the foot of the bed, then leaned forward. Bracing my elbows on my knees, I pressed my temples and groaned.

I unstrapped my boots. I kicked them off. The left flopped onto the hardwood floor by the bathroom door and the right touched down by the closet. One at a time, I put one of my feet across my knee, peeled off the sweaty tube sock, and rubbed them.

"Oh, yeah. That's it." I pressed my lips together, working my thumbs between my toes. "Mmm . . . "

Bart nestled up beside my hip.

I almost wanted to stretch out with him on the bed, but the night was far from over, and I had a load of casework to finish.

Getting up, I stripped. Bart followed each article of clothing that I tossed around the room. After I unhooked my bra and took off my panties, I glanced over at him. He was pawing the fur behind his ears back.

"Is that all I get? I don't show off my ink to just anyone."

Bart's whiskers twitched and his expression said *so what*.

I traipsed into the bathroom.

I unzipped my overnight case. Rummaging through the frugal cosmetics and toiletries I travel with, I found the compact. I turned my back to the bathroom mirror and scrutinized my new tattoo in the reflection. The outlines of red irritation were fading into a dull mauve.

The back piece was derived from a photograph shot by a *National Geographic* photographer. They intended to publish an issue focused entirely on AIM and the Sioux legends held in high esteem by the council. Unfortunately, National Geographic was forced to kill the story. The FBI and the United States Marshals Service claimed that the pictures and the chronicling of the Sioux, especially those mean and vagrant Lakota, put their ongoing criminal investigations at risk.

A bunch of bureaucratic assholes.

Rather than leaving his hard work stored and forgotten, the photographer donated the dozen rolls of film that he'd shot to the res. Specifically, he entrusted them with the only person on the res that had a knowledge of photography. Even though she was six months pregnant and just two months shy of her eighteenth birthday, my mom took the white man on a rugged and treacherous hike throughout our Indian land. She shared sacred Sioux history from her heart. The black and white prints she developed and her narration on micro-cassette tapes are stored in a safe at my loft.

Covering my mouth to suppress a weepy sigh of grief, I bowed my head and lowered the compact. When the waterworks lessened to a few drops, I sniffled, then brought the mirror back up to admire the tattoo some more.

Bordered by a dreamcatcher, the masterpiece depicted my mom, Mina Crow Bear, looking out over the prairie. Rubbing her full belly with one hand, as I undoubtedly kickboxed in her womb, she shielded her eyes with her other hand from the high, scorching Badlands sun. She was watching an eagle soaring in the sky.

If I rolled my shoulders the rocks on my scapulae shifted into a three-dimensional scale.

I put the compact away and ran a bath. As I listened to the water filling the porcelain tub, I moved across the room to the door. I got my cell phone out of my inside jacket pocket. I unlocked the iPhone and checked my voice messages.

Twelve were from Matt.

I scrolled past them, and held my thumb over the message from Unknown Caller. I played it.

"Hey, Leslie." It was Ali. "I finally took your sage advice." She laughed, her voice dropping into a husky octave that always made the skin on the back of my neck tingle. "I've moved to the Pearl District. Call me up, girlfriend. I need a guide to show me the finest vegan dining spots in Portland. Hugs." She ended her call with a big, wet smooching sound.

I heard the pitch of the water getting louder. I tossed the phone on the bed and trotted into the bathroom. The glistening surface was rising just a few inches below the edge of the tub. I turned the water off.

I reached down to pull the plug and drained some of the bathwater. The band of eagle feathers on my forearm, each one a symbol of the warriors in my family languishing in prison for nothing more than fighting for our beliefs and human rights, expanded and stretched underneath the ripples.

The first Crow Bear was a fearless warrior. When he was lying wounded in the snow following the Wounded Knee massacre, a bear came to carry him away and a screaming eagle showed them both the way home.

My family name should've been Eagle Bear, but a white interpreter mistranslated eagle for crow. Bear was a piece of my identity that I surrendered after my exile from the res.

Placing my toes into the steaming water, I planted

one foot firmly on the safety mat, then lifted my other leg over. I eased into the warm embrace to prop my head at the end on a plush, rolled up terry cloth towel. I breathed. I relaxed. The bar hop sweated out of me.

I lathered up. The complimentary soap bore a fragrance of lemon grass and mangoes. The over-crowded nightspots melted away into a secluded beach in Brazil, maybe Costa Rica. Places I might retire to brought on a swelling wave of bliss.

I soaked a washcloth and scrubbed my hands off. The cloth turned black. I wiped numbers off my skin.

To blend into a girl bar in Valencia, I entertained a lesbian that flirted with me. Searching for love with drooping eyes that were more intoxicated than seductive, she'd scrawled her name and number down on my palm. Pursing my lips, I scrubbed harder at the heart she'd drawn by her name.

I dunked my head under to bring myself back to reality. I reemerged and spit a stream of soapy water. Bracing my arms on the sides, I stood up and got out of the tub.

I patted my skin dry with a large beach towel and swiped the steam off the mirror. After blowdrying my hair, I ran a comb through it a couple times, then pulled a bathrobe on. I didn't bother tying the belt.

Going barefoot back to the main room, I operated the Keurig coffee machine to brew a mug of java. While I waited, I got my tablet, Bluetooth keyboard and DSLR out of my bag, and set them down on the desk that faced the stained-glass window. I heard the Keurig hiss. Hovering over it, I inhaled the potent Guatemalan aroma.

I pined for the basement at Green Beans.

Opening the mini-fridge, I pulled out a pint of milk. I poured it into the bowl from the kitchen, and placed it on the floor for Bart.

No sooner had I grabbed my full mug and moved toward the desk than the cat leapt off the bed. Lengthy body stretching, the nimble creature crept up to the bowl. His tiny pink tongue lapped up the nourishment.

"You're welcome, you little shit."

He ignored me and kept drinking.

Sitting down at the desk, I took a sip of the black coffee. The hot liquid warmed my soul that felt dismal after a long night of shitty work that I knew to be beneath me. I put the mug down and set up my gear to sort out the photographs I'd taken, and to type up a report for the client.

I inserted the memory card from the DSLR into the adapter for the tablet. Over two hundred images populated the compact screen. Releasing a long sigh of exertion, I swiped through the photos. I tapped the Music icon and selected an alternative playlist to improve my mood.

I traced my index finger along the bottom of the screen to scroll to the end of the pictures.

An overhead closeup shot that I'd snapped from a third floor fire escape revealed Gavin Steinberg making out with his male friend, before they went down on each another.

At the girl bar in Valencia, I'd followed their girlfriends to the restroom. The redhead was pawing the brunette's tits before they made it inside a stall and shut the door. I crept into the neighboring stall.

A sweater, bras, panties, the redhead's blouse and skirt littered the linoleum. I listened to lips smacking and moaning. While the brunette sat on the toilet, the redhead spread her legs. She started to bang a palm or a fist against the stall.

I kneeled down. Taking a huge risk of being spotted, I held my smartphone below the barrier at an angle. I thumbed a dozen shots with the flash and the shudder noise off.

The redhead's leg closest to my wrist shifted; probably to ease a cramp or for deeper penetration. Holding my breath, I snatched my hand away before I brushed her ankle. The girls never saw me. Their eyes were closed or rolled upward in ecstasy.

Steinberg's fiancé fucked the redhead with a dildo. The redhead's orgasms erupted into screaming that rattled the AC ducting. Joan Jett wailing *Cherry Bomb* from the mosh pit outside hushed up their orgasms.

Investigating whether a wealthy politician's son was being roped into nuptials had reduced me to a low-rent loser shooting smut. I felt low. I'd seen transients rummaging through a trash can by a bus stop near the library earlier. Their disgusting act of survival paled in comparison to this case.

On my tablet, Björk was singing *There's More to Life Than This*.

"Christ, I certainly hope so. I really do."

I couldn't wait to see Matt's expression when I told him what'd happened. Then we'd have to inform the senator. Wearing a skirt suit and heels into that meeting would be easier than informing her of my findings.

Maybe we'd be able to just drop the case and refund her deposit. I knew what the stubborn, hard-nosed detective in Matt would say. 'Turn down a state senator? Are you crazy? Do you know what that'll do to our reputation?'

If I gave my partner the benefit of the doubt, perhaps he'd view the situation the same as me. I hoped he did. I'd heard of long-term partnerships dissolving from lesser conflicts.

A person's sexual lifestyle is no one else's goddamn business.

Maybe Steinberg's mother ought to know the truth; not this way though. She needed to hear about it straight from the source. Her son needed to tell her, instead of Matt and me delivering an 8x10 envelope stuffed with explicit photographs.

"*Fuck* this case."

Putting the tablet to sleep, I stood up to make another cup of java.

As I waited on the Keurig, I paced around for a bit to help calm down and to focus, then walked over to the coat closet by the door. An additional bathrobe and extra hangers were hanging inside. An ironing board was propped up in the corner. An iron and a portable safe occupied the top shelf.

I'd secured Ursula Ivanovich's moleskin journal, and the generous cash advance her uncle had paid, inside. Standing on the Golden Gate Bridge earlier, the mere thought of an investigation into human trafficking, and where it might lead, had overwhelmed me with dread. Now, I felt my skin tingling.

I got a pair of Latex gloves from my go-bag. Setting the bagged journal down on the table, I sat back down. I snapped the gloves on. I broke the plastic seal. Bringing it up to my nose, I sniffed. A nauseous odor rushed up my nostrils. I dropped the bag on the table to turn my head away.

"Oh my God . . . "

Vomit spewed up my esophagus. I swallowed the acidic tang down. The stink the book discharged reminded me of a porta-potty in sweltering July heat. Not even the incense that'd been burned in the room could mask the smell.

Breathing through my mouth, I seized a deep breath. I clutched the bag and dumped the journal out. The eight-by-five book hit the surface on its spine, then landed front cover up. The frayed purple band that kept the volume closed snapped loose. The moldy, mildew-peppered pages leafed open, then shut.

I opened the journal back up. The book had been

written in so much that the pages lied flat without curling up. I flipped through them. English and Cyrillic script were written around doodles and sketches. The words were jumbled up.

"Just perfect," I grumbled. "It requires a code key to decipher. Thanks for sharing that little tidbit, Ambassador."

I hovered over the journal and flipped through the contents, thumbing landscape photographs with my tablet. The flash strobed.

Halfway through, my eyes widened. I stared at a rough sketch of the cement silos on Southeast Twenty-Second Street near the mailbox where her journal had been dropped. The long shadows she added to the structure hinted at her frequenting this location at night. I flipped a few more pages and stopped at a double-page spread marked with bloodstains. Seven portraits of oppressed, sad young women, ranging from seventeen to twenty, stared up at me. Like a photographer, Ursula had focused on rendering their eyes so that their lost souls pleaded to be found, yearned to go home.

I turned the page. A muscular arm flexed, accentuating a tattoo on a bulging bicep, an ace of spades with the symbols in the upper and lower corners substituted with the Marine Corps insignia. Inside the center spade an ominous skull leered frighteningly. It made me think of a Special Force's tattoo. His arm was pulled back in the foreground, about to backhand a girl.

Once I finished preparing a digital copy of the

journal, I resealed the evidence, and put it back in the safe. In the bathroom, I pealed the gloves off, tossed them in the trash, then scrubbed my hands with soapy lather under hot water.

I moved back into the main room. The opening guitar riff from Pearl Jam's *Once* blared on my iPhone. It clashed with U2 on the iPad. Bart jerked awake from his sleep. He meowed like I had some nerve, then sprung off the bed and ran out through his cat door. I used the tone for new e-mail notifications.

Who'd be sending me an e-mail at this hour? Matt preferred to call or text me. Anyway, I imagined right now he was stuffing singles in strippers panties or getting his nipples pinched if he left a good tip. It was probably just an advertisement or spam that didn't filter to my junk folder.

Picking up the handset, I unlocked it and checked my inbox. I opened the new message.

Gavin Steinberg wanted a copy of the group photo I'd shot.

Like any dedicated entrepreneur or workaholic, Steinberg's digital signature included his mobile number.

I double-clicked the home button and swiped over to the phone. I tapped his number out on the screen.

"Let's get this over with," I said.

A mouth breather picked up on the third ring. "Hello."

I spoke up over the treadmill whirring in the

background. "Is this Gavin Steinberg?"

"Yeah. Who's this?"

"I'm the photographer from the tour. I just got your e-mail."

"Oh," Gavin said, "hope I didn't wake you."

"Nope. In fact, I've been going through the pictures and there are several good ones of you and your friends. I'd like to show them to you in person. How about now?"

"Can you e-mail them to me?" he asked.

"No offense," I said, "but I don't know who sees your mail and not all of them are for public domain."

"No problem," Steinberg said. "We can meet somewhere for breakfast in the morning."

"I have a flight to catch at 9." I lied.

He paused, thinking, weighing his options.

Come on, Gavin, I thought. *You know you want a memento of you and your boyfriend walking through San Francisco; a hi-res image too, not just another rushed selfie. You can't pass up this opportunity.*

"Brandi Apartments," he said. "580 McAllister. Make it fast."

Putting on a clean pair of black Levi's and a red tank over a charcoal sports bra, I retrieved my boots. To insulate myself against the cold night air, I opted for a dark blue flannel shirt. Pocketing my keys, I slipped my Leatherman tool in its sheath on my cargo belt, and snatched my helmet.

I stopped at the door. My body felt light. Realization

hit when I reached around to touch the small of my back.

I missed packing my Glock.

Locking my room, I hustled down the stairs. The college student at the check-in counter was asleep. She snored and mumbled numbers.

I jogged outside. The address Steinberg gave me sounded vaguely familiar; recent, even. Throwing a leg over, I sat on the Streetfighter and fastened the helmet straps under my chin. By the time I twisted the ignition key, I remembered 580 McAllister.

The engine thundered between my thighs and I rushed off. Traffic seemed thin. I cruised northeast along Market Street for a little over a mile, then turned left onto Franklin. Fog was beginning to take shape. The Streetfighter's headlight penetrated the pockets of mist clearly, making last-second deceleration or swerving through detours unnecessary. I arrived in under nine minutes.

I couldn't find a parking space near the U-shaped building. I coasted right onto Redwood Street between the rear of the apartments and the state office building that occupies the rest of the block. I spun around where the alley dead ended. Stopping the bike underneath a patch of trees in the far left corner by a row of dumpsters, I swiveled the kickstand down.

I removed my helmet and got off the bike. Setting the helmet on the seat, I approached the gated entrance to the walled-in courtyard behind the apartments.

Tilting my head, I took in the gargantuan palm tree

that rose up in the center of the courtyard; one could travel past the front of the building and never know this tree existed. Its vibrant evergreen leaves fanned the shadows around the lit-up grounds. The moist wind gusted, shaking the large leaves; a banner hung from a streetlight advertising *San Francisco Noir City Film Festival*.

I traced a finger down the columns of last names listed on the intercom mounted by the gate. I pressed the button by *Steinberg*. The round speaker squelched.

"Who is it?" Gavin Steinberg asked.

"It's the photographer."

"Third floor," he said, "room thirteen, in the back."

The lock in the gate clicked. I pushed the iron entrance open. Before I stepped through the threshold, I spotted a person's silhouette in a third-story rear window watching me. As I made my way down the concrete path, I saw them turn around and back away. To my right, a high retaining wall erected out of white brick kept the palm tree and other shrubs decorating the grounds contained. Crickets were chirping a lullaby.

At the back door I pressed another button. The magnetic lock fixed to the top of the door hummed and detached. I opened the door and walked inside.

Turning left, I moved through the hallway until a sign led me to the elevator. For a structure built in 1912, it was well-maintained and didn't smell musty. I got out on the third floor and stayed to the right until thirteen showed up in immaculate gold fixtures on a door to my left.

I rapped three times. Light shifted through the peephole as the occupant checked me out. I heard the deadbolt tumblers grind and turn.

Gavin Steinberg opened the door and bid me welcome with a head shrug. I entered his place, a modest one-bedroom cave of about eight hundred square feet. Steinberg was wearing sweats and a 49ers tank. He wiped his neck and arms down with a towel. His skin glistened with sweat. I noticed the treadmill I'd heard earlier was folded up, stored in a roomy closet in the corner.

"Isn't this building great? I'm glad you're getting a closer look. Perhaps it'll make an interesting sidebar in your art book," Steinberg said.

"That's right," I said, "Dashiell Hammett used this place in a Continental Op short story."

It was mentioned during the tour.

"*The Whosis Kid*." He tossed the towel over his shoulder, then waved a hand at a couch along the wall to the left of the closet. "Please, take a seat. Can I get you something to drink? Bottled water, coffee, hot chocolate?"

My lips curved up into a faint smile. "No, thank you."

As I sat down, he went for the fridge tucked away in a nook by a small dining room table. A microwave and a drip coffee maker sat in the center. "Well, I'm going to get a drink."

"If you have something stronger," I said, "you might want to pour yourself a double."

He chuckled. "Why?"

Cracking the seal on a bottle of *Aquafina*, Steinberg guzzled the liquid down. He stepped over to the couch and sat on the far end away from me. By either drinking too fast, or maybe just from clumsiness, he gagged. Water streamed from the corner of his mouth and shot out through his nostrils.

I leaned forward with concern. "You all right?"

"Yeah, yeah," he said, coughing. "It went down the wrong way. Don't get any closer, please. I probably stink."

This is nothing. I photographed you giving your boyfriend head.

"I'm not just a photographer," I informed Steinberg, then faced my iPhone display toward him.

He saw the picture I'd taken of him performing fellatio. Cupping a hand over his mouth, he jumped up and swerved around.

Bracing both hands on the edge of the kitchenette, Steinberg dry-heaved.

I heard chunks spatter the sink. I moved to the fridge and got another bottle of water. I set it down on the counter by his hand, then returned to the couch.

The vomiting stopped. Steinberg yanked the towel off his shoulder. He wiped his mouth off before turning around to face me.

Jaw clenching, he said, "Who the fuck—"

His eyes closed. He took deep Zen breaths and his lips counted. After reaching ten, Steinberg opened his eyes. "Do you know who I am?"

"Your mother hired me," I said. "I've got a PDF copy of the contract on me to prove it."

Steinberg and I had a heart-to-heart chat. We discussed the senator's reason for putting Matt and me on the case. Less than thirty minutes later, I presented the best course of action in my most reasonable, compassionate tone.

"Tell her the truth, Gavin."

"What about you and your partner and the pictures you've already taken?"

"I came down here for other reasons," I said. "As for your mom's case, we'll refund her money and eat the expenses. I'm certain that Matt will make the same courteous and professional choice here."

He stood up and paced around.

"I can give you a week to figure out what you want to do," I said, "then I'll have to present my findings to the senator. If you tell her about this conversation, the deal is off. Do you understand?"

He was looking out the window, down into the courtyard. "Is that him?"

"Huh . . . ?"

"Your partner," Steinberg said, nodding at the view below.

Bolting off the couch, I trotted over to the window and peered over his shoulder.

I saw one of the guys that'd tailed me the other night, the bald one, smoking a cigarette and loitering on the street side of the brick wall. He stood in front of the gate for a second, rattled it like a drunk that'd forgotten where he lived, before strolling back behind the barrier. I clipped my iPhone back into the holster.

"Listen, Gavin. No matter what happens, stay here."

"Why? What's going on? That isn't your partner?"

"No, it isn't. You're about to see a real-life Continental Op throw down," I said, then dashed out.

I jogged down the corridor. When I reached the elevator, I noticed the door to the fire stairwell and pondered taking them instead. In my blood-boiling, provoked state, I'd be too apt to trip and break something. I pushed the button to call the elevator. The floor indicator dinged and lit up immediately. The door parted open.

Ponytail's face elongated in surprise as he reached out with both arms, his gloved hands stretched like talons, to grab me.

The motherfucker wrapped his arms around air. I ducked, then charged, tackling him. We smacked into the rear rail of the elevator. Driving a combination of elbows into his stomach, I pounded ripped muscle. He grunted in pain, breathing in short bursts to withstand the pressure. I drove a fist upward, aiming to smash his jaw.

He tilted his head back at the last second. My haymaker missing only served to piss me off more.

Clutching Ponytail's coat collars, I rammed a knee up into his crotch.

The next time you piss, it'll be through your armpits.

A blunt pain shot through my knee. I mashed my teeth together to hold in a yelp.

Ponytail latched onto my shoulders and jerked his head forward. The dull ache from the solid head butt pulsed through my skull. He shoved me down onto the floor.

"Cup, bitch," he said.

Grabbing a handful of my hair, Ponytail pulled me up. I threw a wild hook at his throat. He batted it aside, then yanked my hair back, hard. I cried out.

"Sounds like me at the store. Now we're even. Where's the journal?"

"What journal?" I blinked.

The sadistic expression on his face sagged with disappointment. Waving his index finger, Ponytail clicked with his tongue. He jerked down on my hair again. I winced.

"I'm going to enjoy showing you what I do to liars, b—"

I locked my arms behind his back, then jumped in his grip and pulled him upward and over. Ponytail rolled upside down, his wingtips breaking one of the light fixtures. The fluorescent tube rained sparks. I pinned his hip down with my knee. The elevator shimmied.

He moaned and groaned.

Stuffing my hand into my pocket, I withdrew my

key ring. Ponytail opened his eyes in time to look up at the nozzle of my pepper spray canister. I sprayed a concentrated stream into his face.

Ponytail kicked his legs like a crab flipped on its back and raked his eyes. He yelled in Ukrainian. Standing back, I thumbed the number-1 button. As I felt the car lurch to take us down, I stretched a bit. I flexed my knee; it felt fine. I realized the sleeve of my flannel shirt had torn during the scuffle. I took the shirt off and dropped it on Ponytail's head.

The door opened. A woman in a fast food franchise uniform freaked and dropped her bag of groceries. I stepped over the rolling contents and walked out of the elevator.

Going around the tenant, I pointed a thumb over my shoulder. "Rapist."

She nodded frantically and went for the stairs, putting a flip phone to her ear.

The elevator closed on a bottle of water and Ponytail's muffled moans.

Pocketing my keys, I sprinted for the rear entrance. I kicked the crash bar and stormed outside. I threw my other knee up, scrambled on top of the short retaining wall, and trotted across the courtyard. The fresh air enhanced by the palm tree and the other shrubs was tainted.

The cigarette smoke from Ponytail's accomplice puffed up like a chimney. It gave up his location on the other side of the high wall. That, and he coughed.

I increased my speed. An oak bench provided me a boost. Right hand purchasing the top of the outer edge, my left hand clasped the inner face as I vaulted over the wall.

The stocky thug spit his cigarette out. His thick arms shot outward and his loosened tie flapped in his face, caught in a rolling breeze.

My riding boot heel bashed his sternum in. A gasp exploded through his lips. Q Ball tumbled backwards, smashing the blacktop with his spine.

I landed on both feet.

Q Ball rolled around from side-to-side, hands clutching his chest and wheezing. Ah hell, maybe my surprise attack exasperated a heart attack.

Walking up to him, I stomped on his cigarette, as it just happened to be in my path, then loomed over him. I watched Q Ball closely for a minute. He didn't appear to be turning blue or purple. The veins in the whites of his eyes weren't rupturing from a lack of oxygen.

I returned to the Streetfighter. Opening one of the storage containers on the back of the bike, I got out an extra-large zip tie. I strolled back over to Q Ball.

He'd managed to roll over and get up on all fours. He made a noise that sounded like a cow in labor, then pushed himself up on his knees.

I secured his wrists behind his back. Grabbing a double fistful of his yellowish white shirt collar, I bent my legs and exerted my thighs to haul the fat ass up.

"On your feet," I said, then a screeching sound of

tires on asphalt echoed from the mouth of the alley.

I looked ahead and flinched.

Ponytail, in the driver's seat of their Charger, passenger's window rolled down, had come to a parallel stop at the alleyway entrance. With his left eye closed, both lids swollen red, Ponytail's bloodshot right eye wobbled as he looked down the sight of a suppressed automatic pistol.

Huddling behind Q Ball midway down the short alley, I heard the slide click-clack against the hammer. The shot went wide and the slug embedded the courtyard wall; brick fragments scattered. Ponytail cursed and pulled the trigger again. I didn't see where it went. I was too occupied holding Q Ball still as he squirmed and whimpered.

Ponytail yelled his lungs out and started blasting wild. I heard a bullet ricochet with a high-pitched whistle and a streetlight shatter. My helmet hit the ground and wobbled. A couple shots pinged the dumpsters. Q Ball let out a howl. I breathed in the thick haze of cordite, it stinging the throat. Q Ball jerked against my braced arms and gurgled. He began to convulse. I wanted to plug my nose at the stench of excrement his bowels purged.

The gunfire stopped. Peeking over Q Ball's slack shoulder, I squinted up the alley, and through the gun smoke, at Ponytail. He was shaking the Beretta. He threw it to the floorboard, put the Charger in gear, and rocketed north up Franklin.

I shoved Q Ball's bullet-riddled corpse down.

Running back to the Streetfighter, I mounted the motorcycle, donned my helmet and started the engine. I toed into high gear and raced after the Charger's exhaust trail.

I turned east onto Golden Gate. The Charger's taillights weaved through light traffic, running a red at Van Ness. Accelerating to give chase, I changed my mind and slowed down to a crawl. A police cruiser at the southeast corner, emergency lights rolling and squawking, made a right turn and pursued the Charger for me.

Heading north on Van Ness, I turned right onto McAllister and double-backed to the Brandi Apartments. I stopped at a red light. Sweat dripping down my face, I craned my head around to look up towards Redwood Street. The police hadn't arrived yet, but I was certain that the tenant outside the elevator called them.

I considered coming forward. The law would be on my side. After all, my actions were justified. There was no point in denying or obfuscating what happened. If a crime scene technician worked the elevator and the alley thoroughly, my prints would be lifted and identified.

I didn't think an investigation would even go that far though.

Once the tenant stated that a woman fled the scene after taking down a sexual predator, they'd move on to the body in the alley. When the police connected his death to the gun in the Charger, they'd nail Ponytail for the shooting. Case closed.

Keeping the Steinbergs separated from this bigger case also influenced my decision to lay low for a while. If at all possible, I wanted to avoid that kind of collateral damage.

In the morning I'd phone my attorney and check my logic with her.

Two things I knew for sure: Ursula Ivanovich's journal was worth killing for, and San Francisco wasn't safe anymore.

SIX

Brown, shaggy hair unwashed and unkempt, matted by the showering rain, Alec Winter entered the Ardor strip club. The clean-cut face of the Silicon Valley software executive had metamorphosed, seeking refuge in the anonymity of a metropolitan underground. He'd grown a mustache and goatee, too. Winter and his companion, Antonio Mercer, sat down at a vacant table near the stage. To the untrained eye, they were just another pair of slobs looking to get in from the dampness and enjoy a night of adult entertainment.

Mercer, a dishonorably-discharged Gulf War Marine and former medium-heavyweight boxer- turned-bodyguard, grinned at the strippers like a teenager ogling sports cars. He wanted to take one for a drive, open her up on the highway, and see how fast she'd fly. With his shaved head and Slavic attributes, including prominent cheekbones, he bore a slight resemblance to Yul Brynner. Fight promoters dubbed him the Wild Card. Word on the streets was Mercer had gotten kicked out of boxing for using steroids and gambling.

"I've got the munchies," Mercer said, unfolding the food menu gently, as if he didn't want to rip it apart with his massive hands.

Winter couldn't speak. His jaw was hanging. He stared up at the stage. The stripper was integrating a yoga stretch into her dance routine.

"I'll have the veggie platter with spinach hummus," Mercer said.

"Good choice," the Goth waitress in fuck me pumps chimed. "What do you wanna' drink?"

"Two pints of PBR," Winter said. He watched the petite minx hip-walk away. "I love me the curvy proportions of *P-Town* girls. Plenty of meat on their bones and more ass to ride than . . . Hey! You spot a cop or something?"

"I want what he's getting." Entranced, the boxer's square-shaped bald head nodded at the front of the dive.

Winter glanced at the lounge chairs lined along the walls.

A brunette African American in leopard-print lingerie rode and slid around on the lap of a mangy, thirty-something, punk that looked like a stage diver out of a Nirvana music video.

"Don't worry, remember that pole dancer at Union Jack's gave us discount coupons for lap dances here," the software programmer explained, before his eyes bulged and mouth fell open. "Holy shit . . . I think she's dry humping him."

The punk traced a finger up the dancer's thigh. He also said something that made her flip her head back in laughter.

"Dumb ass." The boxer snorted through his crooked nose. "I bet the bouncer tosses him out."

Sideways from the rim of his glass, Winter glanced at the hulk of a bouncer at the bar, while a shorter one carded customers at the entrance. Neither one of them intervened.

"Thirty-six / twenty-three / thirty-five. . ." Mercer groaned at the stripper, tilting his head sideways to get another angle of her supple curves. "Wow."

She braced her hands on the punk's shoulders to snuggle in against his crotch. As she started to sway to and fro, her shoulder length curls curtaining the course spikes of the kid's buzz cut, his hands gripped the plush arms of the lounge chair tight. When her hips began to grind harder, she unhooked the whip coiled at her waist.

Unfurling it with a flick of her wrist, she then braced the back of the punker's head to pull his face into her breasts.

"Shit," Winter said, spilling some beer down the front of his flannel jacket. "Not even the dancers in Bangkok touch a man that much."

The three-song set ended. After the punk slipped a fifty-dollar bill into the dancer's panties, he headed for the restroom. The back of his frayed T-shirt read *I ❤ Boobies*.

When the grungy hoodlum returned from the john, Mercer intercepted him.

"My friend would like to buy you a drink." His Russian accent faintly bled through his guttural speech.

"Thanks," the punk said. "Maybe later. I'm busy. Hey, Sandra." He offered a pair of twenties to the Goth waitress. "That offer for a dance still good?"

With a thick smile accentuated by gold hoops pierced through her plump black lips, Sandra undid her apron, grabbed the punk's hand, and pulled him to a couch.

Shoulders slumped, Mercer retreated to the table. "Guy's not interested. Can't say that I blame him."

Winter dug into his pocket and withdrew a roll of cash the size of a baseball. He peeled off a pair of fifties and tossed them at Mercer.

"Palm him these," he said, then flinched at the screams of an orgasm from the Goth stripper.

The punk didn't turn down the green. He joined Winter and Mercer at their table. The stripper had to go back to the bar and serve other patrons, but she made up for her absence by getting three others to take her place. Four rounds of PBR led to tequila or vodka shooters, phone number exchanges, and enough dirty sexual innuendo to make Doctor Ruth blush.

The strippers flashed dreamy eyes at Mercer,

listening to his gruff voice. They also loved fondling the tattoo on his bulging bicep. It was simply the face of a playing card, the ace of spades. Closer inspection revealed the symbols in the upper and lower corners were substituted with the Marine Corps insignia. Inside the outline of the center icon an emerald-colored skull grinned with devilish pleasure.

The waitress didn't do too great a job of keeping the empties cleared off the table.

While a redhead escorted Winter to a couch and proceeded to show him more than her peek-a-boo tattoos, the punk smuggled himself to the bathroom and unlocked his cell phone.

●

Matt Grudge

I was the punk.

"This is Matt Grudge," I said, kicking the stall doors open to make sure that they were vacant.

An awful stink turned my head away. The commode in the first stall had plugged up. A thick porridge of feces and sewage had flooded the bowl up to the rim.

At least I was alone. Earlier, I'd walked in on the sounds of a pervert in the farthest stall masturbating.

"Yeah, yeah, the Grunge Operative. That's me."

For now, I focused less on that bullshit nickname getting under my skin like a bad tattoo, and more on tightening the collar.

"Listen. You know that delinquent father and

software designer, Alec Winter, the one that owes two years of child support? I've got him wrapped up at the Ardor strip club. No, he's not going anywhere. The dancer I set him up with has a fetish for handcuffs."

"Watch him close. I'll get units rolling right away," the non-emergency woman dispatcher said, then disconnected.

I detected a hint of single mom pride and urgency in her tone. She was going to enjoy making those calls. A victory for abandoned mothers everywhere.

Even though my clients had forged a fake identity to give me misleading information, more research I dug up about Winter's real ex-wife, Stacie *Durant*, indicated he was delinquent in paying child support. Feeling pretty damn good and successful, I called Leslie. I got her voicemail.

"Leslie, we got Winter. See you to—"

A left-handed fist clenching a scalpel rested on my left shoulder.

"I took a sip of your beer by mistake," Mercer said, his gravelly voice marred by sour breath and an acidic rasp. He lisped pronouncing 'mistake.' "Clever, using dead soldiers as a spittoon for your shots all night. I came in here to clean up after blowing chunks all over a stripper. I overheard you springing your pathetic little booby trap. You shoulda' barred the door shut with the janitor's doorstop after you stepped in here, like I just did. Was that your partner that you just called?"

My eyes widened.

"Don't look so surprised, Grudge. I've been enjoying watching you make a total fool of yourself. Not as much as I'm going to enjoy beating you until you beg me to break your neck. The crime scene cleanup boys will have to squeegee what's left of you off the walls. As for Leslie Crow, I know she's returning from San Francisco. She aided in eliminating two of my business associates down there."

I smarted off with a sympathetic sigh. "Well . . . efficient help is hard to find."

As he admired himself in the grimy mirror, Mercer's lips curled up into a sadistic grin. "I'm looking forward to mounting her scalp on my trophy wall."

Knocking Mercer's left wrist up with my shoulder, I dropped into a crouch and elbowed him in the bread basket. I spun around. As he doubled over groaning, Mercer's jaw and his own body weight collided with the fierce right uppercut I drove upward. I kicked him in the groin to put some distance between us.

It drove him back maybe three steps. My solid blows merely seemed to stun the massive son of a bitch. He grunted, straightened up, squared his shoulders, and moved in.

Aw, hell . . .

He was squeezing the scalpel so tight, the implement seemed to be a grafted appendage between his thumb and index finger. Sweaty fear oozed down my face. The blade swung across my nose. It swooshed through air as I pulled my head back.

I misjudged my proximity to the mirror. My skull cracked the glass. Pain vibrated down through my neck and shoulders. Disorientation jumbled up my senses.

Mercer's right hand grasped my throat to hold my wobbling head steady. He pulled his left arm back, preparing to run the scalpel through my eye. "I spy . . ." he cackled.

The point of the surgical knife glimmered, then thrust at my vision in a blur.

I grabbed his wrist with my right hand. As Mercer's other hand began to tighten on my windpipe, I reached around my back for the liquid soap dispenser. I gagged to breathe. My fingers searched, clawed at the faucet fixtures, then finally found the flat lever. Pumping a generous glob of soap on my hand, I smeared it around Mercer's hand gripping my throat.

He lost the chokehold. Shaking my head to clear a few stars, I sunk my left fist into his abs, then crooked my arm in to drive an elbow into his jaw. Blood smeared my forearm. I twisted around to put my back to him.

Mercer wrapped his right arm around my chest. His bicep possessed the strength of a python. With a long grunt, he wrestled his left arm, bending his elbow, and leveraged the scalpel toward my face.

I butted his nose with the back of my skull. Mercer shouted in pain. His right arm loosened.

Lifting my legs up, I braced my feet on the edge of the sink and shoved us back hard.

We flew backwards past the stalls and the urinals.

Mercer's back rammed the door. The wood frame splintered around the hinges.

I pushed his left fist straight up. We stepped a wild dance around the grimy, piss-stained checkerboard-patterned tiles. I jockeyed him over to the first stall.

I bashed his left wrist against the edge of the stall arch, all the while applying strong pressure to the bundle of nerves there. His fingers opened. The scalpel plopped into the backed up toilet.

Grinning at myself in triumph, I left my body wide open for Mercer's second wind to erupt. He drove a flurry of combinations into my torso. In an act of desperation, I held my forearms up to protect my head.

I kicked him in the shin. Off balance, Mercer's shoulder telegraphed the swing at my head. I ducked and charged.

The door gave away.

We rolled out of the foyer and onto the floor of the U-shaped lap dance area. A couple of the strippers screamed. They hopped off their patrons and ran. Several of the dancers just shrugged off our brawl and kept grinding and writhing. Meh, they'd seen blood and teeth on the floor before. A blue-eyed blonde unsheathed a droid phone from her thigh-high boot and shot video.

Mercer landed on top. He punched me in the face. The flesh around my right eye started to swell. He hit me again.

Throwing my legs up, I scissored his head with my feet. I strained and tightened my thighs. Breathing deeply to muster one-hundred percent of my remaining strength, I lifted him up off me an inch-at-a-time.

His arms flailed, throwing blows at me that swiped through air.

I unlatched my foot and drove a kick into his sternum.

Mercer flopped backwards and smacked the floor spread-eagled. His hand landed next to a serving tray a waitress had dropped, next to broken bottles and a corkscrew.

Blood-tainted spittle dripping from his lips like a wild dog, Mercer lurched toward me as I attempted to stand up. My exhausted legs gave out, knees hitting the ground. Mercer raised the corkscrew up over his head to poke a twisted hole through my skull.

"Hey!" Natty shouted over a vicious thwack.

The stripper shooting the fight shrieked and dropped her phone.

The tip of the bullwhip slashed Mercer's hands clutching the corkscrew. The bar tool sailed over my head. I heard the length of leather whoosh through the air. Natty was winding up her arm for another strike.

Gripping his lacerated hand, Mercer bolted for the hallway between Natty's office and the dressing room. Natty cracked the whip. She knocked the EXIT sign off its ceiling mount. Sparks flew.

I moved to give chase.

"Stop! Police!" I heard from behind.

"He's rabbiting," a cop said.

"I don't know why they run," another officer asserted.

"No!" Natty yelled. "He's the good guy, you *assholes*."

Tiny barbs snagged my shirt. An electrical charge crackled. The juice shot throughout every muscle and nerve of my body before I could even blink. Nothing left to do but scream.

I slapped the floor, twitching. My teeth chattered an SOS message with the current.

Then I saw light flashes that dissolved into darkness.

SEVEN

Matt Grudge

I came to, one diminished sense at a time. My head pounded as hard as a construction crew hammering in new siding. Inhaling a deep breath, I winced at a twinge that enveloped my ribs. The temperature was too warm. Beads of sweat trickled down my temples and cheeks.

Reflexively, I brought my hands up to rub my sore chest. An ache in my forearms surged upward. I tried cradling them for comfort. My limbs met resistance. The metallic jangling and steel around my wrist inferred I'd been handcuffed. They grazed the scar tissue on my wrists from being hung up and tortured at Dee-Dee Magnolia's farm.

I wriggled around on my back. The contoured leather cushions I was lying on eased the pain. I opened my eyes gradually. I could open and squint through my left eye without my pain threshold dropping. A mere flinch of the right one though drove an agonizing spike of misery through my skull.

I tasted traces of blood and turned my head side-to-side. It was elevated on a fluffy pillow. This situation was a huge improvement from the treachery Pepper had dealt me. Still, the restraints didn't help my disorientation any.

Pretending to be unconscious, I listened to the bite of quarreling voices.

"Two weeks!" Natty said. "Two weeks is like a beach town closing down for Independence Day weekend. What right do you have to close me down that long for?"

"Ardor's now a crime scene," Captain Glen Hart informed. "You're lucky. The D.A. could use this incident to shut you down permanently, Natty. He's got plenty of conservatives on his platform to do it, too."

"Fuck him," she said. "What crime scene? People get in scraps here all the time."

"Your place has a room tucked away beside the bar for private dances," Glen elaborated. "We found a patron by the name of . . . Alec Winter and one of your dancers in there. Your bartender gave us the girl's stage name, Jade. Her throat was slashed and the guy had foam seeping through his clamped mouth. Cyanide probably."

My eyes flinched at this revelation. No way Mercer had enough time to silence his compromised principle and slay the stripper, possibly one of my anonymous clients, before our encounter in the john. That meant an accomplice, or possibly another killer, saw their opening and took it.

"That's just great!" Natty said. "You assholes identify the pervert, but you don't bother to tell me one of my girl's is dead."

A door slammed shut.

"Do you want me to bring her back, Captain?" an officer said.

His voice matched the one I'd heard just before the electricity incapacitated me.

"No," Glen said, "let her go. Go get one of the bouncers though. Maybe they can help operate this video surveillance software to find the footage of the murderer."

The door unlatched, then closed again.

"Can I be of some help with that?" a woman said.

"Heather . . ." Glen said, sighing wearily. "Stay where you are. I don't need a detective on leave handling evidence. The only reason I sent for you is to help sort through Grudge's bullshit. He'll find it harder to lie in front of a beautiful woman that's been following him around Portland's seedy nightspots."

"Gee, Glen," she said, her tone on edge, "that really speaks to a high regard for my investigative technique."

"So does the wallpaper on Natty's computer screen,"

the lead detective said. "Tell me, how much did that lap dance cost? What did her lip gloss taste like? Hopefully it doesn't get back to your fiancé. And by the way, when addressing me in the company of other cops, suspects, or witnesses, it's *Captain* Hart."

"I told you, *Captain*," the woman argued, "I'm certain that Grudge paid for the lap dance to lose me."

"Spare me the semantics, Detective. Is he awake?"

Soft fingertips delicately lifted my eyelids. I stared straight up into the face of the hot blonde that'd followed me around the other night. A few strands of her frizzy, bed-head hair swayed over me. *Nice highlights,* I thought.

"Why you sneaky little shit," the woman detective said, then squeezed my nostrils closed.

I gasped for air and sat up quick. The cop released my nose.

I peered around the room. We were in Natty's office, on the long couch that took up almost the entire length of the wall to the left of her desk. Under her purple leather jacket, the detective had on Oregon Duck sweat pants and a jersey. Glen sat in Natty's chair, hunched forward at the computer monitor. The backlight enhanced the rudely awakened scowl on his face below a slanted fedora. I was surprised his trench coat wasn't frayed more. Glen had clearly thrown his clothes on in a hurry.

"Computers suck," Glen said, then leaned sideways to yank his coat aside and unclip the walkie-talkie from the side of his belt. He thumbed the "push-to-talk" switch hard. "Jim, when you're done processing the private room, we're taking the tower hard drive out of the owner's office."

The brash captain of homicide for the downtown division stood up. He returned the radio to his hip. Stomping out from behind the desk, Glen scooted one of the chairs that faced the art deco structure around to huddle with me and his detective.

"Welcome back to the land of the living, Matt," Glen said. "What were you doing here tonight?"

I gave him a brief account of the case to locate Winter. I mentioned how elusive my supposed stripper clients were at communicating with me. This led me to asking Natty for help tracing Winter. I didn't drop Maxie's name, bring up her violent past, or her recent falling out with Natty. Unless Maxie showed up holding a knife, all of that seemed circumstantial. I wrapped up my summary.

Glen rubbed his round chin, processing the information. His detective scowled at me.

"Oh yeah, I almost forgot," I said. "Yes, I paid the stripper to give your rookie detective here a lap dance. I needed to get her off my tail."

"Well," Glen said, looking at me, his detective, then back to me again. "I appreciate your cooperation and honesty. So, I'm going to cut you a little slack, Matt. Let this case go."

"Mercer knew I was coming," I said. "I'd like to know why. He also accused my partner of interfering with his people in San Francisco. Which makes no sense to me at all. She's just there to conduct a background check. Completely unrelated."

Hart sneered at my grungy appearance. "Mercer's training saw through your facade, obviously. We've talked about this before. Have you been able to talk to Leslie?" he asked.

"No."

Glen mumbled that he'd check with homicide divisions down there, scribbling shorthand on a notepad the old-fashioned way. "Don't make this personal. You don't know the full extent of the danger you're wading into. Not to mention this case is one victim away from becoming a federal investigation. I'll suspend your license if I have to stop you."

"My partner is a stubborn person," I said. "You know that. I'm going to need more than 'it's too dangerous,' or 'pulling our tickets' to convince Leslie to sideline this case."

"Mercer isn't your run-of-the-mill bodyguard, Matt. Wild Card didn't come from his boxing days. It was his code name. He ran a special forces outfit during Desert Storm. The scuttlebutt from my old friends in the Corp is that Mercer was caught torturing an Al-Qaeda prisoner at Guantanamo."

"Why isn't he rotting away in Leavenworth?" I asked.

"He's efficient at prison escapes," Glen said. "Not to mention this psychopath has enough confirmed kills to populate a small town cemetery. You're lucky you're still breathing."

"As for you, Detective MacGraw . . ." He pointed his index finger at her. "Go home, unpack, and settle into your new home. It'll help get your mind off nailing Mercer and the sons a bitches holding his leash. Promise me you'll do that. I don't need the first woman detective under my command becoming that next victim."

Legs crossing, MacGraw's intense, competitive 'game on' expression melted into that of a demure, sensible woman's whose lot in life was to get pregnant, raise rug rats, and cook meals in the kitchen.

"Okay, Captain," MacGraw said. "I promise."

I knew an insubordinate rebel lying through her clean white teeth when I heard one. I was beginning to like her.

"Good," Glen said. "Now will the both of you get out of my sight. I've got an investigation to run."

I held up my wrists and shook the cuffs. Glen called me a smart ass under his breath and unlocked the restraints.

MacGraw and I got up off the couch. We left the club. I caught site of Natty hugging a body bag on a gurney beside the medical examiner's van. She was bawling. I started to head over there.

MacGraw latched onto my wrist. "She'll be alright. Can we drive someplace and talk about this?"

"In that restored '68 Mustang of your's?" I said, visualizing the YouTube clip Natty had forwarded me. A radio station helicopter broadcasted live footage of

Heather's *Bullitt* car chasing down a rape suspect.

"Sure."

I walked with the detective to her vehicle parked near Dante's lot. "What's with the Oregon Ducks apparel you're always wearing?"

She unlocked the passenger side door with a key. "You tell me the stories about your tattoos, I'll fill you in about my wardrobe preference. It'll have to wait though."

"For what?" I asked, watching her sashay over to the driver's side.

"Until after I hire you for a job on the periphery of this double murder," MacGraw said.

I folded my arms and leaned them on the roof of the green Mustang. "My caseload is pretty-well booked up, Detective."

"Call me Heather," she said, then ducked inside the Ford classic.

Pulling the seatbelt across my lap, I clicked it secure. I marveled at the pristine interior. The only modern touch I noticed was a dock mounted on the dashboard for her smart phone.

Heather fastened a racing harness around her curvaceous figure. Sticking the key into the ignition, she turned the engine over. The V8 engine hummed with precision.

"It's only fair that I tell you something about me up front, Matt." She shifted into reverse. She licked her lips. "I can be very persuasive."

Pulling out onto the street, the Mustang's tires rolled so smoothly the fastback chassis seemed to float across the asphalt.

Focusing on the road through the cascade of water being brushed aside by the wipers, Heather gripped her steering wheel at ten and two. She maneuvered a few blocks west, then cruised south down Broadway. Night lights blinked or shadows swirled across the hood and the windows. Her coordination alternated between steering, working the pedals, and shifting gears as if she'd been surrounded by cars instead of dolls all throughout her childhood. Anticipating other motorist's courses, she adjusted hers to swerve around them at the last second to keep moving.

Brake lights blinked or glowed steadily, coasting along or slowing down near the curbs. This late on a weekday evening, the only traffic in our path were taxis prowling for fares, or tourists returning to their hotels. Handfuls of pedestrians were gathering on the MAX train platforms on the north and south side of Pioneer Square to commute. Heather knew the timing of the traffic lights and matched her speed. We barely stopped once, and that was for a snuggled-up couple taking all the time in the world to cross an intersection.

"You and Glen must go way back," Heather said.

She'd picked up on how he'd allowed somebody dressed like a punk to address him by his first name in front of one of his police officers. I scratched a mark in the plus column for my opinion of the blonde detective.

It would take more than a tight bod and paying attention though to get personal information about my friendship with Glen.

"Yeah," I said, "we've revolved around some of the same circles."

Heather giggled. "I can't quite picture the captain jumping up and down in a mosh pit at a Pearl Jam concert."

"During his senior year at Portland State he dyed his hair cobalt blue once," I said, recollecting how we'd first met.

It'd been over a beer funnel at a frat party. Some cops are born with that distinctive, authoritative bark. 'One can of beer,' Glen said. 'We're not done yet. Suck, pledge. SUCK!'

Her wide mouth blew apart to laugh hysterically.

I surrendered to the infectious laughter and joined in. My expulsion of air paused after every other comedic burst. My ribs ached. The reminder of innocent times and riding around with a blonde, fit and high-spirited enough to be a cheerleader, boosted my whipped pride.

"What did Glen mean when he said, 'We've talked about this before'?" she asked.

"I used to be just another blue-collar, snazzy-clothed private detective," I said. "A lot of my cases for finding missing runaways or tracing cheating spouses chasing jailbait tail led me to seedier environments, like Old Town." I jerked my head back at the part of downtown we'd just left. "No one would talk to me. So, I altered my appearance and approach to the job. Glen thinks it's just a useless gimmick my age is going to catch up with someday." I shrugged. "The name of the agency on my office door, and the clients that keep walking through it, keep disproving him though."

"I see Glen's point," Heather said. "You're kinda going gray on the sides."

I pretended to ignore that comment and looked out at the night.

We crossed the Ross Island Bridge. To my right, the glass towers in the South Waterfront district glowed. I could make out the black steel cables of the aerial tram that stretched from the base of one of the dignified skyscrapers, up to the main Oregon Health & Science University campus in the Marquam Hill neighborhood. A light shroud of fog swirled around the isolated forest of treetops on nearby Ross Island.

U.S. 26 turned into Powell Boulevard. We passed the Lucky Devil Lounge on the left where Heather and I had first caught sight of each other. "Where are we going?" I asked.

Please, God, not another strip joint.

She decelerated and pulled into the lot for the Original Hotcake House. An old-fashioned sign advertised: *Open 24 Hours, 1/4 Lb. Special Hamburgers*. The yellow awning above the front of the aqua colored building also read steak. I knew what Heather had in mind.

"I'll buy you breakfast," she said.

"They say the easiest path to a man's heart is through

his stomach."

"Relax, handsome," she said, wiggling the massive stone on her engagement ring at me before unclipping her racing harness. "It's only your thoughts I'm after. Besides, you're shaking a little. I figured you could use a bite to eat. Calm some adrenaline."

Stepping out of the Mustang, we headed for the entrance. Heather jogged to get underneath the awning and out of the pouring rain. Hands stuffed in my jean pockets, I looked both ways before I walked between the rows of parked vehicles. The cool drenching cleansed my body of the debauchery from bar crawling.

Heather wrinkled her face at me. "Get out of the rain you idiot."

I grinned up into the downpour, then held the door open. "Who's the lucky guy?"

"An architect who makes more money designing buildings in Brazil than I do fighting crime," Heather said.

We entered the greasy spoon. On an antique jukebox Buddy Holly and the Crickets crooned. Heather and I scanned the crowded joint for a vacant table. Heads turned, taking notice of Heather's buxom, athletic figure. Three bikers in riding leathers huddled together and devouring stacks of pancakes took a break to ogle her rack. Hash browns on the end of some guy's fork fell into his lap. A young woman vying for her boyfriend's attention, as he stared at Heather, gestured at her boobs and cried out, "Hey, I'm right here."

A busboy finished clearing off a table near the swinging door to the kitchen. We hustled over and sat down. The waitress beat us to the table with glasses of ice water and menus. Her intricately coiffed purple hair dangled around bare shoulders. She wore a blue tube top sweater, slashed acid-washed jeans, and lime green Keds.

I chugged the liquid down and asked for another.

"Sure thing, sweetie," the glam-punk waitress said. "Coffees?"

"Black," Heather and I said in unison.

After our java arrived, Heather dumped six packets of sugar in her cup. The hot brew soothed my throat, sore from strangulation. She ordered a farmer's market vegetable omelette, hold the dairy and the potatoes. I opted for a ham and cheddar omelette with extra cheese and a side of hash browns.

"Got it." The waitress finished jotting down our orders. Her long fingernails were painted hot pink and every single one of them featured Hello Kitty in glitter. She shifted away between tables.

Another pretty face I'd seen someplace else recently, but couldn't remember where.

Heather caught me looking, thinking. "Need a wingman?"

I set my mug down gently. "After all the strip joints I've staked out over the last couple nights, it's actually kinda nice to see attractive girls with clothes on."

"I think you did a good job on that stakeout," Heather

said. "It couldn't have been easy, staying focused with all those naked girls prancing their assets around."

"You mentioned a case," I said.

"What do you know about the Tabor Strangler?"

"Rapist preying on joggers," I said.

"That's all?"

"I told you, my caseload's been full lately."

"Three victims," she said, holding up her fingers.

Scar tissue lined Heather's hands. Her bubbly personality and flirtatious nature more than compensated for the ugly brand. I wondered how she got them, but held off asking just yet. The detective was buying me a warm meal. Listening seemed the least I could do.

"All women, late-twenties to early-thirties," she continued. "Different ethnicities and employment backgrounds. Raped, then strangled with rubber tubing."

I sipped my coffee. The hot brew soothed my split lip and my tenderized gums.

"I bet Glen breathed a sigh of relief at this not being a serial killer," I said.

"Why all runners then?" Heather said. "And all dumped on or near public parks."

"There's another commonality, obviously," I said.

"About a week ago, I helped apprehend a suspect involved with the killings. She'd just abducted a forth victim."

"Wait a minute. *She?*" I said, intrigued by the uncommonality. "What do you know about her?"

"Not much. My insubordinate behavior apprehending the bitch locked me out of the case," Heather admitted.

The regret and pride she'd just swallowed was probably a lot more bitter than the coffee. She took a sip to wash it down. Her gaze drooped with embarrassment. It didn't diminish the twinkle set deep in her eyes to see justice served.

It's an obsessive trait I've seen looking in a mirror.

"Maybe checking the victims' financials will dredge up a lead," I said.

Heather sighed and the intense expression on her face sagged into a pathetic one. "Come on, Matt. How could rape and strangulation be about money? This is about anger and power."

"Where did the women work? Were their hobbies looked into? What about a social media angle?" I asked, the determination in my voice eager to prove that approaching me wasn't a useless mistake.

"Two college students, one from PSU, the other a drop out from Mount Hood, and the paralegal investigator worked for a civil action firm. As for their extra-curricular activities or online interests, I haven't the faintest clue."

I almost broached if she'd heard anything about the autopsies, but the waitress arrived with our orders. The heaping plates clinked on the table as she set them down gently. I inhaled the savory aroma of butter, sharp cheddar cheese, ham, green peppers, and strong onions that rose up in the steam from the hot plate.

"Mmm . . . " I said. "Smells delicious."

"I'll be right back to refill your coffees," the waitress said with a grin and rushed off.

After smothering my golden brown hash browns with ketchup and Tabasco, I shook enough pepper onto the omelette until the yellow turned black. I cut a sizable chunk out of the fluffy texture. Oozing cheese melded all the layers of meat and veggies together. Shoveling a bite into my mouth, I felt my tastebuds buzz.

Heather sliced into the top of her bulging omelette. The medley of veggies inside spilled out. She stabbed a huge mushroom, spinach, a few olives, and egg with her fork. She chewed her nibble of food at least thirty times.

Meanwhile, I was cutting into my third. It wasn't that I wanted to hurry up. The night's events had left my appetites famished.

Heather loaded her fork back up. "See. I knew you were hungry."

The hot food reinvigorated my thought process. "How did your suspect lead you to my stakeout, Heather?"

"Now that's a superb question," the cop replied with her mouth full. She swallowed and added, "Before Glen and the crime scene—"

"Beg your pardon," one of the bikers interrupted. A few hairs of his full beard were stuck together with traces of maple syrup."Is your name Heather by any chance?"

She looked up at the stout rider. "Yes it is. Do I know you from somewhere?"

As he pulled his gloves on the leather creaked.

Shit, I thought, *probably an ex-con on parole she'd put away.* While I mentally prepared myself to engage in another brawl, I stopped eating and just smiled. An uncomfortable silence lingered.

"Homecoming," Heather finally said. "My freshman year at OSU."

"Yeah, yeah!" the biker said. "You cheered at my game! We lost. What are you doing now?"

"I'm a police officer," she cooed. To make the encounter even more awkward, Heather reached into her purse and displayed her shield in her palm as if it were a priceless family heirloom. "Isn't it *shiny*?"

"Well, good to see you." The biker rushed off.

Heather didn't wait until the guy was out of earshot to comment, "If you'd have focused more on the football than my tits, like you still do, maybe you'd have won. Interesting, isn't it, how some people never change. Points for you though, Matt. You haven't stared at the girls once."

I was looking over my shoulder. The rider kept walking.

He probably didn't hear her on account of the chatter levels around us getting louder and our waitress cleaning a nearby table. Porcelain dishes and silverware clattered. It explained the Oregon Ducks gear Heather liked to wear.

"Cheerleader, huh," I said.

"Don't put me in a box," she cautioned.

Polishing off my omelette, I wiped my mouth off. I gestured up-and-down at my raggedy appearance. "How could I?"

"Where were we?" Heather asked.

In the corner of my eye I saw the biker bragging to his gang. He pointed towards Heather and made big boob motions on his chest. "You found out something about the suspect you apprehended before Glen took charge of the scene."

"Right," she said. "I couldn't disturb her body for ID. So, I checked the glove compartment instead. An assortment of glittery and neon matchbooks fell out. I snatched some papers and leafed through them fast. The registration didn't give me a name. Instead, I got a company called Real Solutions. They're a payroll service based out of San Francisco, with satellite offices spread out all up and down the West Coast. The matchbooks, by the way, all came from local strip joints."

"That's a solid connection," I said. "Why tail me from bar-to-bar though? You're a competent homicide detective. What do you need me for?"

The bikers started their choppers. The roaring engines vibrated the windows. I leaned in closer to hear. I noticed Heather's silver dangling earrings were footballs.

"Your rep proceeds you," she said. "I needed to know if you're a real P.I., not just a con man or a phony my colleagues snicker about. So far, you haven't disappointed me. Besides, I stick out in strip joints. I can't tell you how many times the bartenders and bouncers kept asking me if I wanted to audition."

"Alright, Heather. What's the angle you need me to investigate?"

"Real Solutions used to operate an office in Southeast Industrial, out of a warehouse on Second Avenue west of Stumptown Liquidators. I checked with the real estate company that owns it. From time-to-time they rent it out. Law enforcement or fire companies conduct drills, roller derbies hold competitions, or party planners throw raves."

"Sounds like a real den for evil," I said.

Sliding her plate aside, Heather pulled a checkbook out of her purse. She unclipped the green and yellow Ducks pen from the spine, clicked it, opened the book, then positioned her hand to write.

"You know what, call it good old-fashioned female intuition," Heather said, "but I need to know if something shady goes down there in the next few days. Maybe there's a link to the Tabor Strangler. If there isn't, then we'll have eliminated a dead end. I'll pay you at least three-nights work to stake the place out. How much?"

●

Heather tapped the brakes at the corner of my

parking lot. The Mustang jerked to a stop. I unfastened my seatbelt and reached for the polished door handle.

"Thanks for breakfast and the ride," I said. "I'll check in with you later."

"Wait a sec, Matt. Where's your phone? I'll give you my personal number. You can call me if you need backup."

I reached into my jacket pocket, withdrew my cell. I thumbed the Wake Up button. The screen remained dark.

"It's dead," I said. "Don't worry about it. I'll find you. As for backing me up, I've got a partner."

Heather's lips pursed and her eyes rolled. She grabbed my left hand. Unsheathing a pen from the visor, she held my hand steady, and began signing her name and phone number on my palm.

"I understand that," she said. "I also know how dull stakeouts can get. I'm going to be bored out of my head myself, unpacking, figuring out where I want to mount my cheerleading trophies and mementos. Leslie might be on another case. You can call me up. I'll talk your ear off and help keep you awake."

Finished scrawling, Heather blew on my skin to dry the ink.

"Do you have something against business cards?" I asked.

She let go of my hand and tossed me a smile. "Yeah, they're too easy to throw away."

I got out. The horses revved up and she sped off. The

rain had let up.

Too energized by the night's endeavors, too stoked about acquiring a new client, I went out for a drive in my autumn gold collectible, a 1962 two-door Impala hardtop my grandpa willed to me. I stopped at the Bank of America ATM on Morrison to deposit Heather's check. The machine spit out my receipt. A proud feeling of success rushed through me at seeing the revenue for Alternative Investigations remaining in the black.

My instincts buzzed. I visualized all of the cash exchanged at strip joints.

Stuffing my wallet in my back pocket, I hustled back to the car. I cast looks over my shoulder with a paranoia I hadn't felt in a long time.

I thought about Pepper. I wondered what she was doing now to evade arrest and to survive. I shuddered from a chill that started in my neck, then fired down to my feet. If our paths ever intersected again, I didn't know if I'd feel relieved, or a need to satisfy vengeance by putting a bullet through her head.

I still felt an attraction to her, too.

I rested my forehead on the wheel.

There was no reason to harbor positive feelings for a bitch who'd betrayed me. Especially since I'd already met someone else.

After leaving Soy Toy the other night, I'd dropped Ali off at her place, a swank tower of condos behind Powell's Books. We didn't exchange numbers. As I watched her rush inside the building, I knew I wouldn't see her again. A British model seemed way out of my league.

Lifting my head up, I cranked the 409 on, then headed over to the Safeway on Thirty-Ninth and Powell. I loaded up a shopping cart: a case of Coke and bottled water, energy drinks, assorted snacks for the stakeout, a couple bags of Water Avenue coffee, a tin of breath mints, and a bag of ice.

I stowed the bags in the trunk. Getting back in the car, I headed downtown.

A brittle cold front was blowing in. Frost crystals were forming on the streets and sidewalks. I hustled inside my office.

After setting the sacks down on the coffee table in the waiting area, I pulled my denim jacket off and hung it up on the coat rack in my space. I saw a strand of cobwebs attached to my old trench coat and dusty fedora. A wolf spider the diameter of an eyeball crawled back into its hole.

Moving behind my desk, I turned my HP laptop on. The hum of the old hard drive sounded like a rusted harmonica.

Opening Google Maps, I brought up a satellite view of the three-story warehouse Heather wanted staked out. I anticipated obstacles in my way. Trucks hauling trailers through that industrial sector could obfuscate any surveillance. The storage facility next door may've been patrolled by security guards. The top floor of Stumptown Liquidators across the street would be a strategic spot to set up a stakeout nest. I'd worked for the owners before, conducting background checks. I sent them an e-mail.

Rapid knocks banged against the outer office door. Getting up from behind my desk, I stepped sideways up to the door. At this ungodly hour, a night visitor could be dangerous. I looked at their shadow through the frosted glass. The curves appeared feminine and junior-sized.

I unlocked the door and cracked it open. Once I saw who my visitor was, I yanked the door open all the way.

"Ali." I couldn't suppress the surprised tone in my voice.

"I can't believe I'm standing at your door either." Her high alabaster cheeks blushed scarlet. "Can I come in? We need to—Your face! How did you get beaten up like that?"

Sidestepping, I swept my hand inward. "Nothing to worry about."

Ali marched into the room. Unwrapping a scarf that doubled as a hood, she unbuttoned and removed her heavy, navy blue coat. She flung them on the sofa, then began to pace back and forth. No purse. Why did she race over to my place in desperation? She ran fingers through her hair to loosen it up. Yoga pants emphasized her sculpted thighs and the outline of her labia majora. Her sports bra was soaked through with water and her taut nipples pushed firmly against the cotton. The soles of her sneakers stamped treads in the carpeting.

"You must be freezing," I said. "Can I make you

some coffee, or tea?"

She turned a screwy expression at me. "I can't sleep. The last thing I need is caffeine. Besides, you Americans can't make tea to save your life. It's either too bitter, sour, or too sweet. No offense, hon."

"None taken," I said. "What's keeping you awake?"

"You."

"How's that?" I asked, stepping away to lean my buttocks against the front of Leslie's desk.

"How the *fuck* should I know," Ali said, gasping in between deep breaths. "You're just a scruffy, courteous fellow that gave me a ride. Maybe it's how you're one of those strong, silent types. You didn't talk a lot about yourself. You're mysterious. I like that. It's sexy. I want to know more about you."

I picked up on the rhythm of her speech pattern and finished her thought. "But . . ."

"When exercise didn't get you off my mind," Ali said, "I Googled your name."

"What did you find, Ali?"

"Leslie and I go way back, Matt. We grew up with Dee in San Francisco. I don't know if you and I can sustain a relationship with Leslie as your partner."

"I'm sorry about Dee-Dee. I understand where you're coming from," I said. "And if you want to end this fledgling relationship before it begins on account of your friendship with Leslie, it's okay. On the other hand though, we're consenting adults. Leslie's a grown up also. I want to see you again."

"Thing is, I'm not into a monogamous relationship," she told me. "I tried one recently and it backfired. Right now, I'm keeping my options open."

"My job doesn't afford me a lot of extra-curricular time to put into a relationship," I said. "If at any time I don't fulfill your needs, you can walk away. I won't take it personally."

She stopped wearing out a trail on the rug. Taking one last deep breath, Ali exhaled as she walked over to me. We stood toe-to-toe. She placed one hand on my waist, while her other hand twisted the button on my jeans.

"So, friends with benefits is a lifestyle you're able to live with, huh. Sounds too good to be true," Ali said. "What is it about me that makes you willing to accept that?"

"I've always harbored a fondness for self-assured women."

"How are we going to break this to Leslie?" Ali said, rising up on her tiptoes.

Her puckered lips were getting closer. I inhaled cinnamon on her breath; my favorite spice.

"Whenever you think the time's right, we'll take her out to dinner and tell her together."

"Where is she now?"

"On a job in San Francisco," I said. "She'll return tonight."

"Then she won't barge in and disturb us," Ali said. Her skin radiated a glow.

I shook my head. "What do you have in mind, gorgeous?"

"Fulfilling your fantasies. Pleasure," she said. "Parts of me I want your hands on."

Ali pulled the sports bra over her head, then ripped my Hawaiian shirt open. The bamboo buttons flew all over the room.

"Hey! That's my fav—"

I kissed her as she pressed her hardened nipples against my chest, and wound her arms around me tight.

EIGHT

Leslie Crow

My key hit the lock early. Turning the deadbolt, I heard the tumblers snap. I entered my loft, then dropped my go-bag. It thumped on the hardwood floor by the coatrack.

"I love that sound."

I unzipped my black leather jacket, peeled it off and hung it up. My greasy hair stank of exhaust. I stepped up into the kitchen. Setting my helmet down, I fingered the jagged ding made by a nine-millimeter bullet.

Emptying my pockets, I tossed my keys and coins down by the cordless phone. They jangled into the cerulean blue ceramic coin dish I'd gotten a few years back at Saturday Market, Old Town's renowned, seasonal outdoor bazaar.

I opened the fridge to grab an Arrowhead. Guzzling the ice-cold water down, I killed the bottle, then chucked it into the recycle bin. The plastic bounced off the rim and the bottle tip-tapped on the floor.

On my way to the bathroom, I pulled my clothes off. I didn't give a shit where they landed, either.

After showering the road trip off my skin and out of my hair, I marched into my bedroom. Pulling my mom's granny square quilt back, I lifted my knees up onto the queen-sized mattress, then texted Matt.

I'm back. Need a nap for a couple hours. Wake me up and I'll slug you.

I silenced my phone and plugged it in the speaker charger on the headboard. Pulling the quilt up, my head fell back on the pillows. I closed my eyes, but sleep didn't come.

Breathing deeply, I waited a few minutes for lucidity to kick in. The storm of unrest in my soul wouldn't subside.

How many people were being sold into slavery through the human trafficking pipeline that'd burnt Ursula Ivanovich to death? *Sleep on that.* Turning on my left side, I bartered with myself that I needed a little rest before beating the streets for answers.

My iPhone vibrated on the headboard. I picked it up. The display indicated G. Christie, Esq. was calling.

I swiped to answer, "Hey, Gillian. I just got home. What's—?"

"Come to my office. Serious shit's gone down at the Russian embassy in San Francisco and I think it might be fallout from your case for the ambassador," my attorney said. "Put on something professional, a little war paint, and drag that partner of yours along, too."

I wish Matt hadn't fucked her after my birthday party. I'd warned her not to do any tequila shooters with him. Of course he never called her back, either. Not even just for a cup of coffee between adults to sort out that it'd just been another one-night-stand.

"I need to make a pit stop at—"

"Right now." Gillian cut me off again, ending the call.

I jackknifed out of bed. Walking over to the closet, I slid the door open. I unhung a garment bag, swung it onto the bed. Standing on my tiptoes, I reached up on the top shelf to pull down a wide, white shoebox. A thin layer of dust drifted around my face. I set the box down on the bed also. Silver lettering on top of the glossy lid read *Jimmy Choo*.

My nose got too close to the layer of dust on the box. The hairs inside my nostrils twitched. My head jerked back and forth in a sneezing fit. Snatching a Kleenex from the nightstand, I cleared my sinuses. I took another quick shower to shave my legs.

I pulled the skirt suit out of the bag and flicked the lid off the shoebox. Once dressed, I walked into the bathroom. The heels click-clacked a different tone from hardwood to linoleum. I applied just enough makeup to cover up the bags.

In the main room beside my desk, I knelt down and removed the floorboards that concealed my fire safe. Not even Matt knew it existed. Prying the lid up, I placed

Ursula's journal inside with my mom's photographs and a few priceless mementos from the res; this hiding place would have to do until I could secure Ursula's accounting in a safety deposit box.

As I set the wooden boards back, I felt a sting on my thumb. I sucked the splinter out. At the door, I paused and turned around for a moment to admire the peacefulness of my place.

I opted taking the elevator instead of the stairs. Out on the street, I walked along the sidewalk on the south side of the building. The high heels were already giving my ankles and calves an aching burn. I spotted my Saturn parked up ahead at the curb.

I reached into my go-bag for the keys. Pressing the disarm button on the fob, I didn't hear the double-beep of the alarm system disengage. Great. Dumb ass forgot to arm it. Matt is usually more security conscious than that. Something must've distracted him. I blamed the strip joints.

Ducking inside, I started the engine. As the sedan warmed up, I peeked at the gauges. At least he'd filled the gas tank after his bar crawl. I turned the stereo on. Storm Large perked up my ears and made me feel good to be back.

Pulling out into traffic swiftly, I ran a red light to turn left onto Burnside. I smoked past Stadium Fred Meyer. To maintain speed, I swerved around other motorists commuting home; several of them were driving too damn slow, chatting on their cell phones. My shoulders swayed left and right. Vehicles were jammed up at Twelfth, one of them a police cruiser. I decelerated and strapped on my seatbelt. Fishing my Bluetooth earpiece out of my go-bag, I plugged it in.

I called Matt.

His voicemail greeting droned.

"I hope you're at the office," I said. "Gillian needs to see us. Throw on something appropriate. I'll be there in five minutes."

Golden rays from an orange-hued sunset were glowing in the rear view mirror. They were absorbed and reflected by the Pittsburgh plate glass and granite face of Big Pink, the U.S. Bancorp Tower, Portland's second largest building. Hanging a right onto Broadway, I glanced at the sign for Mary's Club that featured the silhouette of a burlesque dancer, and wondered if Matt's canvassing of strip clubs had taken him into downtown's oldest strip joint.

●

I barged through the outer office door. Nudging it closed with my heel, the glass panel rattled. I tossed my go-bag down on my desk chair.

Opening a large bottom drawer, I pulled out a purse that matched the suit. I snatched a tissue from an overturned Kleenex box. As I dusted off the knockoff, I perused my desktop.

Everything seemed the way I'd left it. I might be a slob, but the disorder kept my focus on more important things sharp. Like my package from Urban Carry

Holsters that'd arrived.

I transferred a few necessities from my go-bag to the purse. The thought of toting one around made me want to gag. I inhaled a scent of cucumber and honeysuckle that the buildings ancient HVAC system hadn't purged from the air yet. It smelled vaguely familiar.

I flipped the top of the purse closed and turned the clasp. Holding the purse at my side by the handles, it felt dainty and ridiculous.

I noted the spiked bracelet on my wrist, a gift from Matt that commemorated our first meeting and case together years ago. It didn't go with the suit. Screw it. I refused to take it off. The weathered leather and honed points matched my personality all too well. It also gave me hope that my work with Matt as a P.I. would endure.

Turning around towards the wall, I shifted the oil painting of the Wounded Knee massacre to reveal my weapons safe. After twisting the combination dial and pulling the thick door open, I reached inside.

"Come to momma," I cooed. "I've missed you."

I withdrew my Glock 26 and its holster. After setting the compact pistol and the accessory down on my desk, I secured the safe and replaced the painting. Hiking my skirt up, I bent my knee, then rested my heal on the seat of the chair. I strapped the holster around my thigh like a garter belt and tucked the "Baby Glock" in snugly.

I took my foot off the chair. Pulling the skirt hem down to where it stopped just above my knees, I smoothed the inseam around my curves.

"Much better."

I could hear keyboard tapping from the adjoining room. I leaned forward and craned a look through the foyer. I saw the back of Matt's head. He was sitting at his desk, his head bopping.

I drifted into his office with stealthy footsteps. Matt hadn't gotten my message. He wore a hoodie over a T-shirt, faded jeans, and sneakers. Unaware of my presence, he continued to nod his head to the beat. Earbuds were plugged in. The tunes bled out through the air. Nirvana's *MTV Unplugged* album enhanced his focus on research.

LexisNexis filled the scratched up screen of his HP laptop. He picked up a Manilla folder off of his desk blotter.

It was Pepper's case file that we'd opened up a long time ago; back when she'd hired us to find out what her foster parents had done with her life savings. Matt fed her Social Security and bank account numbers into LexisNexis.

Details in the form of news articles and a subpoena about a civil action brought up against a temp agency and payroll service called Real Solutions populated the screen.

Matt cocked his head sideways; maybe he spotted my reflection in the monitor. He wiped his eyes before reading the screen again. He'd been at this for a while. He pointed the eraser tip at the upper left corner of the subpoena record, a name labeled as co-defendant in the lawsuit.

Moving his fingers on the touchpad, Matt clicked buttons and saved the file as a PDF. Scuffed, lacerated knuckles indicated he'd brawled in a fistfight. The backlight in the laptop screen illuminated fresh bruises on his cheeks and his unshaven jawline that clenched.

He scrawled a crude diagram on a blank sheet of stationary: *Pepper/Human Trafficking* inside a rectangle, then *Tabor Strangler Suspect & Real Solutions Payroll/Temp Agency* which he bordered with a box, then dropped a line and an arrow to point to *Strip Clubs/Alec Winter—$*, and drew a circle.

Matt pressed down hard. As he nearly finished completing the flowchart, the graphite tip broke and the wood splintered.

I chimed in, "It's always about the money."

Every muscle and nerve tensing up, Matt let out a short scream. Plucking the buds out, he swiveled around. Papers from Pepper's file that he'd set in his lap, because he'd ran out of space on the desk, slipped off and fluttered to the floor.

"What the *fuck* . . . ?" he yelled.

After taking a good look at me, he stopped and stared. He snapped the pencil in half. His mouth gaped open.

Smirking, I winked and turned in profile to model my executive attire.

"*Jesus*, Leslie," he grumbled. "Don't sneak up on me like that."

Matt stood up. His height rose above me by only a couple inches. Rubbing his thighs to get the circulation flowing, he walked around the room. I fell in step with him like a shadow.

"I sent you a text," I said. "Gillian needs to see us about something that's happened to our new client in San Francisco."

"New client . . . ?" he said, his face contorting with confusion. "The senator's case has been booked for months. How did it go anyway?"

"We'll get to that later," I said. "Listen, the Russian ambassador whose niece was burnt to death in Estacada hired us to expose the human trafficking pipeline responsible for her murder."

"Sacha Ivanovich?" Matt asked.

"That's him," I said, then pulled the collar of Matt's hoodie down to get an eyeful of a blue and purple hickey on his neck. "Who's your new girlfriend?"

"Just someone I met at one of the clubs."

"Stripper?" I asked.

"No," Matt said, perturbed. "Can we focus, please? My sex life isn't open for debate."

"Well," I said, "will you at least wear a turtleneck sweater or a shirt with a big collar to cover that up? I don't think Gillian would appreciate seeing it."

"Calm down," he said. "She won't notice it with all the other scrapes on my face."

"Who kicked your ass anyway?" I asked.

Hopefully, my tone didn't come off-sounding too

eager or—

"Jealous . . . ?" my partner kidded.

"Yes," a woman remarked cruelly from the foyer entrance. "I would've at least given you a black eye."

Shoulders flinching, Matt and I turned around.

"How long have you been standing there?" he asked. "You could've knocked on the outer door or announced yourself."

Gillian Christie crossed through the archway. Wavy blonde hair with honey brown highlights bounced around her shoulders and framed her fair complexion. The tailored cut of her beige skirt suit outfitted her stunning figure, befitting an industrious criminal attorney.

As Gillian floated toward us, I couldn't help but look at her legs. A mid-thigh inseam showed off shapely gams. Competitive running for charities up and down the Pacific Coastline kept them shapely and firm. Whenever Gillian rose to her feet in a courtroom, jurors couldn't take their eyes off her.

If I had great legs like her's, then people would hang on every word I spoke, too.

Another factor contributed to Gillian's stability. Her great grandfather had been a tax lawyer in Boston for a Sicilian crime family that became legitimate with his counsel. Her father was a year away from retiring his commission as a captain in the JAG Corps. Practicing law coursed through her veins.

"Where's the fun in that? I came in at 'sex life.' It

doesn't really matter though," she said, bitch eyebrows slanted flippantly at Matt. A plum shade of lipstick and a thin layer of clear gloss added volume to her lips. "I already know you're a slut."

"It's great to see you too, Gillian," he said.

Vibrant blue eyes glaring at Matt, Gillian firmly grasped her satchel in front of her with both hands before she could slap him.

"Coffee, black," she told Matt, then offered me a big smile. "Leslie, I can't believe it. You're wearing a suit. Sexy girl."

We headed for the small round conference table to the left of the window. As we sat down beside each other I said, "I thought we were supposed to meet at your office."

"My floor is being remodeled and retrofitted to install a new security system," Gillian said. "Construction started tearing down the walls in the offices right across from mine this morning."

"What did the D.A. in San Francisco have to say about me fleeing a crime scene?" I asked.

Matt returned with two steaming mugs of java for Gillian and himself, and a bottle of water for me. He sat down across from us to listen and to observe; not a simple task for him since walnut-shaped eyeglasses with red frames accentuated Gillian's oval face. Matt gravitated to smart-looking women in glasses. It got him off.

I appreciated that he was distancing himself, because

Gillian ran hot and furious when men moved on after using her for sex.

"Took you long enough," Gillian said, taking a long sip. "Stumptown Roasters?" she asked.

"Water Avenue," I said. "Are they going to force me back to testify?"

"He sounded aggravated. Fortunately, Ambassador Ivanovich flexes a lot of strong diplomatic muscle at the bureaucrats down there," she said. "The D.A. informed me, during a brief video conference call this morning, that if I deposed you myself and that you remain reachable for more questions as they need answered, he'd accept that arrangement. Then something terrible happened. Less than two hours ago, right in front of the Russian embassy, seven gunmen dressed up as construction workers and surveyors ambushed Ivanovich's Lincoln. With military training and precision, they wounded or eliminated his security detail. They used C-4 to blow the back door. They took the ambassador. There's been no contact from the kidnappers. Have either of you received any calls from blocked or unknown numbers in the last few hours?"

I said no, then told her what I believed really motivated the abduction. "They're after his niece's journal. He gave it to me to track down the human trafficking pipeline that abducted her. A pair of thugs stalked and assaulted me in San Francisco to try and get it."

Matt's eyes widened as he took a long gulp of his

coffee. He forgot to swallow. The hot liquid scalded his chin.

"Ouch!" he yelped, then wiped his mouth off with the back of his hand. "Holy shit! Tell me you've had a chance to look it over. More importantly, that you've got it stashed someplace safe."

"Well, yeah," I assured. "No shit, Sherlock."

Gillian snickered before asking, "What does the journal contain?"

"The text, including the dates, is written in some kind of code or shorthand. It's going to take a while to research the symbols, find the key and crack the code."

"I know a court reporter that might be able to help us translate it," Matt said.

"Ursula was an illustrator. She drew pictures of locales that she saw, portraits of other girls, and one that'll I'll burn into memory of a man drawing his hand back to beat a girl. There's a tattoo on his arm."

I described the tattoo.

"Anthony Mercer has ink just like that on his bicep," Matt said.

"Who's Anthony Mercer?" I asked.

"The scalpel-wielding psycho that kicked my ass," Matt admitted.

"Did you recognize any of the locations?" Gillian asked.

"The cement silos near Fred Meyer headquarters," I said.

"The Gladstone Street entrance to the Brooklyn Rail

Yard is just a stone's throw south of there. Semi trucks go in and out at all hours hauling God only knows what," Matt said.

We exchanged knowing glances. Freight cars on the railroad and trailers on the highways were a sure-fire method for smuggling anything.

"Where's this diary now?" Gillian asked.

"The original's in a safe place," I said, "and I made a digital backup on my iPad."

"Send me a copy," Gillian said. "The D.A. mentioned that he would like to review it."

"I don't think that's a good idea," Matt advised.

"Why the hell not?" Gillian scolded.

"Because the thugs were on my ass *before* the ambassador even handed me the journal," I said. "The other night when they got the drop on me at Senator Steinberg's apartment building, I had to resort to using one of them as a human shield. Asshole nicked my helmet. Whoever they work for is a ruthless, desperate manipulator."

"It's too dangerous," Matt added. "And if the ambassador had wanted politicians to see the journal, he would've handed it over to the State Department. Instead, he entrusted it to Leslie."

"Don't be paranoid. What if something happens to you or to Leslie?"

"I'll die before I surrender it," I said.

"Be reasonable . . ." Gillian said. "Crucial evidence like that should be preserved for safekeeping. The San

Francisco D.A. won't tolerate it being withheld. He might alter the arrangement, subpoena you back to face charges, or arrange to put you in custody here and now for obstruction."

"There's another piece to the pipeline," Matt said. "If you give us a chance to investigate, it might expose more leads to share. Look, there's already a tie between Mercer's tattoo and Ursula Ivanovich's account in her journal."

"This better be for real, and not one of your cheap stalling techniques," Gillian said, pointing her index finger at Matt.

Matt's bold glare pierced the criminal attorney with a dreadful reckoning. "A stripper died during the course of this case."

I flashed him a penetrating glare of concern. I knew damn well that his mother had been a go-go dancer. Her heroin addiction and overdose had plummeted Matt into the foster system. I accepted his dedication to work this case objectively, as he'd done for me after Dee's murder. I made a mental note to call him on it later, though.

He filled in the details about tracing Alec Winter to Ardor; the brawl with his bodyguard, the mercenary named Antonio Mercer, who also mentioned that colleagues of his had a run-in with me in San Francisco; then Detective Heather MacGraw hiring Matt to stake out a warehouse linked to a payroll and temp agency service that employed the Tabor Strangler suspect and

Alec Winter: both of them dead by cyanide.

I noticed that when Matt mentioned the Tabor Strangler, whose victims were all joggers, Gillian's angry demeanor towards him eased up. She leaned forward, absorbing the conviction in Matt's voice. The animosity in her eyes softened to sympathy.

He continued, "Both Real Solutions and Winter were defendants in a lawsuit opened against them by independent contractors—mostly strippers and tattoo artists—accusing them of embezzlement. Leslie and I were paid to trace Alec Winter for dumping his family. Yes, he was a womanizer that got divorced, but his wife and child have never been photographed by paparazzi or pictured in the media. The name the strippers gave me for his wife ended up being phony. And none of them have contacted me again since I confronted them about not being straight with me about their case. About the only thing I'm certain of is that the common link is money."

"Cash-intensive businesses are an ideal place to launder money," I said.

"Yes, they are," Gillian agreed. "How are you going to prove it?"

"We'll start by interviewing one of the strippers that hired us," Matt said. "Her stage name is Star." He seemed pretty damn sure of the place where she danced. "Leslie, are you up for talking to her while I work the stakeout? I'm burned out on tits and ass."

I nodded. "Fine. Anything to ditch this monkey

suit."

My sigh of relief also acknowledged that maybe Matt was making wise decisions after all. He had to be aware that strip joints were a perfect conduit that could stir up thoughts of his mother.

Gillian's brows relaxed; a tell of her willingness to compromise. "Fine. I'll ask the D.A. to give you twelve hours."

NINE

Matt Grudge

Guiding her out of the inner office, I walked Gillian to the outer door. I tried really hard not to crowd her. This simple courtesy proved to be difficult. She smelled good. It wasn't a fragrance that came from a bottle. I breathed in her earthy scent that exuded confidence and passion.

Our hands touched the doorknob at the same time. Her sexual aura tingled my spine. She pulled hers back as if she'd come into contact with a rodent.

"Jesus Christ," she said, anger rising in her voice. "I know my way out."

"Call me old-fashioned," I countered.

Gillian's knuckles crackled as she gripped the knob. She took a deep breath using her whole body before she turned her head around to acknowledge me with a sneer.

"Then learn how to make a phone call," she said.

"I'm sorry, Gillian."

Flipping her hair, she wrenched the door open to bolt. "Don't be an asshole."

She flung the door shut in my face. The glass pane that bore *Alternative Investigations* rattled. I needed to get that fixed. One day it might fracture to pieces. Leaning my head against the frame, I locked the deadbolt.

I regretted not staying in touch with Gillian after the fling that'd followed Leslie's birthday party in February. I simply couldn't picture myself in an exclusive relationship with an attorney; especially one bold and crazy enough to represent my brash partner. Conflict of interest also posed a bad risk to our careers and professional relationship.

Besides, I yearned for an existence outside my life's work. Maybe a relationship with Ali was destined to fail also, but I wanted to try. I believed that as long as I kept Ali distanced from our cases, a safe relationship could bloom. It seemed possible. Other than growing up with Leslie, Ali had nothing to do with law enforcement.

"Too little, too late," Leslie said, moving from my area to hers.

Opening one of the bottom drawers of the scuffed filing cabinet beside her desk, Leslie withdrew a set of street clothes, all black, and set them down on the blotter. She took the suit jacket off and draped it over the chair, then quickly unbuttoned the blouse to peel it off too. A lacy black bra emphasized her athletic bust and complimented her coffee-and-cream skin.

As she turned back around to rummage through the cabinet again, I caught a glimpse of her new full-color back piece tattoo. I was able to discern a dreamcatcher border and a rocky plateau before Leslie spun around. She glowered at me.

"You really have been spending too much time at strip joints," she said. "This isn't a peep show. Don't you have some equipment to pack up?"

"Oops," I said, hustling back to my side. "Excuse me. Nice tat, though."

"Oh, brother . . ." Leslie sighed. "Shut the hell up."

I grabbed a large camera bag off the bottom of shelves stacked behind my desk. Setting it down on the chair, I loaded it with my surveillance equipment. The zipper on the bag had broken a long time ago, but a collapsed tripod synched through the handles kept it shut.

Leslie called out, "Do you want a piece?"

"No, thanks."

Picking up the bag, I slung it over my shoulder gently. My muscles were beginning to throb with a steady ache. The scrapes on my face and swollen bruises around my eyes itched. I thought about Ali and hooking up with her again soon. It dulled the pain.

"Leslie, you decent?"

"Yeah."

I stepped into the front office.

Leslie had dressed down into a pair of worn-out combat boots, skinny jeans razor-slashed on top of the thighs, a tank top, and a turtleneck sweater, which she hadn't pulled all the way down over her torso, yet.

A glance at the desktop revealed that she'd ripped her parcel from Urban Carry Holsters open.

She was wrapping the five-inch, military-grade elastic belt low around her hips. Leslie fastened the hooks and eyes in front for a smooth and snug fit. A double-edge of silicone prevented slippage. Rugged stitching and ornamental ribbon added durability and a touch of elegance.

Leslie removed a Glock from her weapons safe, ejected the magazine to double-check the load, then shoved it back home with a soft click. She holstered the firearm behind her back at an angle away from her spine, then added three magazines and her Leatherman alongside.

She tugged the sweater all the way down. The puffy weave concealed the outline of the gun.

"Nice rig," I said.

"Thanks. It fits up to four compacts if I really wanted to pack that much firepower. Listen, I know that you don't like guns, but are you sure you don't want one? How about a backup in an ankle holster?" Leslie asked, pulling her duster on, then freeing her thick hair from the collar. "We're dealing with mercenaries here. Mercenaries have no honor, no loyalty, and they fight dirty."

Although smiling hurt, I cocked a grin. "Yeah, I know. So can we."

Leslie closed the safe, spun the dial. She pursed her

mouth in a confident smirk. "Only dirtier."

"How did the case for the senator go?" I asked.

Her smug grin drooped. "Not so well."

She gave me a cursory rundown. I listened intently, grateful that she didn't emphasize the sex encounters. After Leslie finished, I told her that I'd have done the same exact thing. Her actions distanced the human trafficking investigation from the senator and her son. His lifestyle exposed, the media would've over blown it into a scandal that could've jeopardized the senator's political career.

"That's good work, Leslie."

"Thanks," she said, throwing her go-bag over her shoulder. "Hope it doesn't soil our reputation, not being able to follow through."

"I really don't give a shit," I said. "I became a P.I. to expose criminals, not to eavesdrop on someone's sexual orientation. It's no one's business. I regret that the job put your ethics on the line that way. You deserve better."

"I appreciate hearing that from you," Leslie said, her eyes twinkling exuberantly. "Let's get back to work and nail these fuckers."

She headed out. I followed, shutting the door gently and locking it. We jogged down the stairs.

"By the way," I said, "my cell phone isn't working. I think it got hit last night during the fistfight with Mercer."

"How are we going to stay in touch tonight?" she asked.

"I'll stop by the 7-Eleven on Taylor," I said, "pick up

a prepaid phone."

Pushing through the double entrance side by side, Leslie and I turned left. We stopped for the westbound MAX train. A cloud cover that reminded me of cotton candy with patches of mold was rolling in. A few rays from the setting sun penetrated the tattered blanket. As the nimbus clouds swirled, they blotted out the last pinkish hues of sunshine. The storm system cleared its throat. A low rumble echoed.

The pedestrian light clicked to Walk. Leslie and I moved across. My ankle dragged a few paces. As we reached our parking lot, a thunder clap drummed directly overhead. I felt the bass of it on my shoulders. It muffled the beep of Leslie deactivating her Saturn's alarm system.

She opened the driver's side door. Tossing her go-bag on the passenger's seat, she ducked inside and shut the door. I rapped on the window with my knuckles. She cranked the engine on, then powered the window down.

"Yeah, what?" Leslie asked.

"Check in every two hours," I said.

The skin between her brows wrinkled as she frowned and stifled a yawn. "What's next? Are you going to remind me that liquor's off limits?"

"I've got a bad feeling about tonight," I said. "That's all. And I don't like the idea of us splitting up, but we stand a better chance of discovering stronger leads by going separate ways."

"Don't worry," Leslie assured. "Everything's going

to be fine."

"Mercer's bound to make a try for you," I said. "He wants that journal."

"Mercer's a mindless thug," she said. "I'm more curious about who's paying him to procure it. Alright, I'll check in every two hours, but you've got to do something for me, too."

"Name it," I said.

She unlocked the emergency brake and shifted into reverse. "Don't make this case about doing right by your mother, Matt."

The engine roared. Leslie backed out and raced off as I shouted, "That isn't fair."

Stomping to my car, I stowed my gear in the backseat. I fell in behind the wheel and shut the door not a moment too soon.

A strobe of thunder lit up the low hanging nimbus clouds. They unleashed a torrential downpour of thick raindrops.

I started the engine. I let the Impala warm up a bit, while my flaring temper cooled off. I switched the thermostat and the wipers on high.

Twisting the radio dial, I pushed the station select button to the Buzz. Mitch was wrapping up his *News of the Weird* program. Traffic and weather would be up next. Daria's smooth voice purred over the squeegee squeak of the wiper blades, announcing that the Morrison Bridge was gridlocked due to construction.

I maneuvered through skyscraper center, and at the corner of Third and Madison, headed eastbound for

Hawthorne Bridge.

I cruised along the steel grating of the truss. The vibrations conducted through the tires hummed in my ears. About half-a-dozen bicycle commuters in rain suits were peddling rapidly. Wind whistled through the structure. The Impala shimmied. A pedestrian gripping a blue and white golf umbrella over his head in a two-fisted grip stumbled to maintain his footing. A strong updraft wrenched the metal ribs inside out.

Turning left onto Grand Avenue, I checked my blind spot, then swerved into the far right lane. The 7-Eleven parking lot was full. I circled the six hundred block and parked at the corner near Taylor Court Apartments. In the Roaring Twenties, the brownstone housed visiting entertainers; now it was a nesting ground for cockroaches grossing out tenants in rent-controlled studios.

I unbuckled my seatbelt and twisted around to reach into the backseat. I pulled the thermos out of the bag. Stepping out of the car, I looked both ways on Sixth and darted across. Droplets of water drenched my scalp and sluiced down my temples.

Across the street to my left I heard the sounds of wheels rolling and smacking a hard surface. That would be skateboarders honing their agility and reflexes on the runs inside a tall brick warehouse that'd been remodeled into a 24/7 gym. Leslie and I worked out there two or three times a week. We'd watched the downtown fireworks last Independence Day from the rooftop.

I entered the convenience store. After filling the thermos with ice chips at the soda machine, I made my way to the check out counter. I asked the clerk jockeying the cash register for a prepaid smart phone. One of the T-Mobile units.

"Sorry, mister," he said. "We're all sold out. You might try the Plaid Pantry up on Twelfth and Morrison. Unless you want one of the cheap knockoffs."

"No, I've gotta' be able to text and e-mail," I said. "Seems kinda odd to be out of a commodity like that."

"A stripper came in a few days ago and took them all," he said. "Bought a shitload of airtime cards too. Fifty-bucks a pop."

"How do you know she's a stripper?" I asked.

"I've seen her dance," the clerk said. "At Raw Assets and other joints around here. Great rack. Nice and tight. Real girl next door quality. Big bedroom brown eyes."

I flashed back to the riffraff I loathed blending in with during my strip club crawl. It took a great degree of discipline to remain in a cordial mood. I could tell by the cocky slant of a mouth on the kid's face that he was barely old enough to drink what he sold, just another punk-ass kid. I'd know. More than I care to admit, I'm one of them.

"Sounds hot." I humored him. "What's her name?"

He stroked his chin. "Something only an ex-hippie would use. Moon Glow? Sunny Daze?"

I'd seen the fluid in lava lamps form patterns faster than this idiot's memory could ever gel into gelatin.

"How much do I owe you?"

His gaze stared off, either still trying to remember her name or daydreaming about the positions he wanted to do while inside her.

"How much?" I repeated sternly.

"My bad," he said. "Just ice chips? Twenty-five cents."

I fished a quarter out of my pocket and tossed it on the counter. I heard the clerk blurt out the stripper's name as the door chimed.

Star.

Following the kid's suggestion, I made a detour over to Plaid Pantry and bought a disposable cell phone there.

As I left the store, I saw a scraggly-haired dude wearing a tan corduroy blazer laced with cat fur, an untucked Grateful Dead T-shirt, bleached jeans patched up at the knees, and frayed moccasins on his way in. He reeked of sickly-sweet kitty litter. His greasy fingerprints smeared cheese puff dust on the glass.

In kind of a rush, I nudged the guy's shoulder, almost knocking him down.

"Excuse me," I said.

"Easy there, my man," he said, then his voice lowered a few decibels. "Hey. Wanna' buy some weed?"

I get that a lot. It's from appearing younger than I really am and the dingy clothes I wear. The offer didn't bother me a bit. In certain neighborhoods of Portland, selling pot isn't dealing; it's hospitality.

"No. Thanks."

Back behind the wheel of the Impala, I tore open the T-Mobile packaging and activated the handset. I texted Leslie the number. Keying the ignition, I backed out, then turned west onto Morrison. A couple blocks down the street, I passed a strip club I'd forgotten to visit. There were so many.

I felt good about handing the second bar crawl over to Leslie. Her fresh senses would be able to see a clearer track on this laundering setup. I couldn't think straight. And my partner was right: musings about my mother and my origin were fueling my resolve to see this case through.

My old man had picked her up at the go-go bar where she danced. He'd been evading a pair of mob enforcers that wanted him to cook some numbers to allow them to evade the IRS. He refused, so they threatened persuading him with brass knuckles and needle nose pliers. The finance geek hid in my mom's dressing room. He impersonated a casino manager from Vegas, and she seduced him for the bulge in his pants that turned out to be more than his roll of getaway cash.

They spent one night together and he knocked her up.

I drew in a long breath and let my thoughts and feelings of the past go.

Yards away from Seventh Avenue, the traffic light at the intersection blinked to yellow. The tires on the Impala were bald and a pair of headlights were rushing up from the rear fast. I mashed the gas pedal and breezed through.

Heading north on Grand, I drove past rustic bars, quaint coffeehouses, and glowing neon-lit storefronts that occupied brownstones. I smelled a hearty aroma of garlic and tomatoes wafting out from an Italian restaurant. I hung a left onto Stark.

Once I crossed Martin Luther King Jr. Boulevard, one block west, the industrial section of Southeast Portland enshrouded me in its gothic ambience. The final shade of night fell like a black muslin backdrop. An eerie veil of fog smudged out the moon. Vandalism to streetlights killed the shadows that usually pooled at the corners of brick warehouses and poured-concrete factories. The absence of light didn't obscure the gang tags spray-painted throughout the neighborhood. The graffiti warned me to exercise caution.

As I roamed the streets within a five-block radius of my destination, I kept my eyes peeled for parking. Signs that reserved spaces for freight deliveries 24/7 heckled me. At least the rain stopped. I switched the wipers off. About fifteen minutes later, I finally found a spot on Alder, beside a warehouse near Rinella Produce. The concrete structure's color and texture resembled bleached bones.

Getting out of the Impala, I grabbed my bag of gear out of the backseat, then locked the car. I walked east. I moved quietly by a half-a-dozen weather-beaten tents pitched on the sidewalk along the curb. I scrunched my nose up at breathing in a whiff of body odor and overripe pumpkin guts. At the corner, a transient squatted by his rusted shopping cart heaped with possessions under a tarp. He washed his hands in the rainwater streaming through the gutter.

I moved on down Third Avenue. While leering at

a white banner on the side of the brick building to my right that read *Qwest Is Now CenturyLink*, I heard a holler of profanity echo up ahead. I whipped my head around to discern where the disturbance was coming from.

Four hoodlums in thrashed clothes were strutting my way, hooting and hollering. One sported a mohawk. The brass ring pierced in his septum was bigger than his nose. Gold chains attached to the ring trailed up into small gold hoops dangling from his earlobes. The shortest hood was swigging a bottle of a beer.

Avoiding direct eye contact, I walked across the street. I didn't run because wild thugs tend to behave similarly to any animal bred on violence. At the smell of fear, they'll chase you down and tear you to pieces.

"Hey, old man!" one of the gangbangers yelled.

I kept walking, but turned my head to scope them out in my peripheral vision.

"Want this?" the shorter hood asked, approaching the transient slowly, offering the empty bottle.

Standing up, the homeless man reached out with his liver-spotted hand to take it.

The hoodlum wound his arm back to pitch the bottle into the sidewalk. The glass popped. Shards exploded, peppering the transient's cart and his body. He covered his eyes, then fell onto the pavement, curling up into a fetal ball to shield his vital organs.

The gangbangers swarmed around the transient, laughing and spitting. Their bodies jumped up and down as if they might stomp him to death.

As my body was still recovering from getting my

ass beaten by Mercer, I wasn't in a condition to take on all four of them. Maybe I could take out the leader to intimidate and scatter the others, but an ache rippling around my ribs made me think of an alternative response.

I dug my cell phone out. Tapping numbers on the display, I cupped the handset with my hand to muffle my voice.

"911. What's your emergency?"

"A pack of gangbangers is pouring gasoline on tent city. Southeast Third and Alder," I mumbled, then ended the call.

I cut through the lot next to the Pearl Oyster Bistro. The French-Cajun restaurant was housed inside what used to be the Royal Hotel back in the day. Some of their cuisine included frog legs and alligator. A mural for a vodka ad that took up the entire side of the building tempted thirsts.

●

Stumptown Liquidators, a family-owned business, has been a retailer of home and office furnishings for almost four decades. I bought a futon for my first studio apartment here.

I huddled underneath the awning at the front entrance, just as the charcoal gray cloud cover unleashed more rain. Fat raindrops spattered my shoes. The neon *Open* sign in the display window was off. I looked at my watch. They'd closed at 6:00 p.m. Only about fifteen minutes ago.

The lights were still on. Looking up into the door

frame, I noticed that the gated entry hadn't been rolled down yet. I figured that employees were still inside working.

I rapped on the door. No answer. I knocked again and shouted out a long hello over the downpour. Stooping my head, I peeked through the door windowpane. I saw shadows whirling about, then a clerk emerged.

"We're closed," he said. "Sorry. Please, come back tomorrow."

"Tell your boss Matt Grudge is here. I'm expected," I yelled through the glass.

The clerk held up his index finger for me to wait a minute. He dashed off. The small awning kept my head dry, but streams of water cascaded down my shoulders and my back. My breathing fogged the glass. When I spotted more movement, I wiped the condensation off with the bottom of my fist.

A tomboyish woman swaggered up to the door. She wore low-rise jeans rolled up to show off toned calves. An orange and black-checkered long sleeve flannel shirt, open and untucked, allowed the abundant cleavage of her pushed-up breasts to breathe through a beige tank top. The cotton was stained with axle grease, maybe ink. Beads of sweat trickled down her chest and made the authentic portrait tattoo of a Boston Terrier glow. A pork pie hat was slanted between its erect ears. A few curly locks of her silver hair peeked out from underneath a red and white polka-dotted bandana.

Unclipping a key ring from her cargo belt, she unlocked the door. She parted it just wide enough for her pouty lips. "You're late, Mr. Grudge."

I nodded, remembering the owner wouldn't be available to grant me access. But their assistant manager and freight dock foreman, Chrissie Butane, would be on hand to let me in. She'd altered her appearance. The hair color on her New York drivers license was blonde.

"Good to meet you in person, Ms. Butane. Please, call me Matt."

"My boss informed you to arrive before 6 p.m.," she said.

I must've been distracted by Ali putting her clothes back on and missed that line of the message.

"It's a rough neighborhood," I said. "Parking's lousy."

A thunderclap strobed directly overhead and a transformer within earshot boomed. The power in the entire block surged. Chrissie glared, her high cheekbones flushing.

"Get in here," she said, jerking the wooden door open all the way. "Wipe your feet. The floors are being swept and mopped."

"Thank you." I hustled inside and rubbed the soles of my sneakers on the welcome mat.

After slamming the door and locking it back up, she turned around and walked. "Come with me. Hurry up."

I followed her caboose as she sashayed through a maze of furniture on the massive showroom floor. Her right butt cheek bulged.

"You didn't even bother to check my I.D." I said. "Shouldn't your security be *tighter*?"

"Before coming out West, I worked the peep shows in New York. I know how to read a lot of people. No one with ulterior motives gets in or out of this place underneath my radar. Besides, if you're really here to rob the joint, I've got a stun gun in my back pocket I'm itching to use."

We reached a door marked *Manager*. Snapping the keys off her belt, Chrissie unlocked it, then twirled around to face me. I stopped admiring her foxy attributes and stepped back.

"Don't press my buttons," she said, "or stare at my ass, either. That's something from my peep show days I don't miss."

I narrowed my eyes and curled my lips into a cheshire grin.

"I wasn't looking at you that way," I said. "For quite some time, I've encouraged your bosses to hire someone with survival instincts to double as a security guard. Like the way you protected that diplomat's apartment from looters on 9/11."

"They were a gang of xenophobic jackals," she said. "I couldn't stand by while they terrorized a Hindustani family on account of their olive-colored skin."

"How did a stripper find herself at an address like that, anyway?" I asked. "And don't tell me wrong place, wrong time."

"A sick friend and tattoo artist needed me to drop off a package. I owed her for designing one of my tats. She was also a live-in nanny for the Mukesh family. An honest living that breaks even in New York usually requires two jobs."

With the influx of fugitives and refugees flooding the Pacific Northwest, raising the cost of living, multiple jobs were a hard reality that could impact everyone's lifestyles.

Chrissie tossed me a clever smile back and held the door open.

"And if you're expecting me to gush with gratitude for your part in getting me hired on here," she added, "Think again."

Walking inside the office, I set my gear on one of the straight-backed wooden chairs that faced a mahogany desk, then took a seat. The legs creaked. Chrissie shut the door. She plopped down on the plush executive chair behind the massive relic of furniture. Reclining back, she lifted her feet and rested them on the blotter. The thick soles of her purple Doc Martens thumped against the hard surface.

We stared each other down in silence for a minute.

"This doesn't have to be awkward," I said.

"Sure it does." She crossed her heels, then broke eye contact to hide her face behind her boots. "I'm being forced to help an asshole that's rifled through my past."

"Just doing my—"

"Your job," she lifted her feet off the desk to let them drop to the floor, "I know. And I don't care how you dress it up. You make my skin crawl, Grudge."

"Please, call me Matt."

"Formalities aside," Chrissie said, gorgeous eyes squinting and discerning with finality. "You'll *always* make my skin crawl, *Matt*. Let's get this over with."

Leaning forward, she opened the large bottom drawer. She hefted a gray cash box from the compartment and placed it on the desk. As she unlocked the box, Chrissie eyeballed me dubiously. "The cash?"

"Right, right." I reached inside my inner jacket pocket and handed the bills over.

She licked her thumb, counted the amount, then tucked the currency into the box. Closing the lid, Chrissie's fingers moved to secure the lock.

"I'd like a receipt, please," I told her. "For my expense report."

With a flip of the lid, she withdrew a tablet of receipt paper and flopped it on the desktop. She snatched a retractable pen from a cracked mug, clicked the ballpoint tip out, then scrawled the transaction details on the blank spaces. Her handwriting flowed meticulously.

"I gotta' tell you, Chrissie, there's still one thing about the background check I did on you that's got me stumped."

"What might that be, shamus?"

"You took the train from New York after 9/11," I said. "The passenger manifest showed that you traveled with a +1. I couldn't find out who you made the journey with."

"I'm flattered," Chrissie said, carefully tearing my receipt from the tablet. "Maybe I'll be that one case in your files that keeps you awake nights."

Snatching the receipt from her fingertips, I folded the paper in half and tucked it in my jacket pocket.

"Thanks a lot." I stood up, picked up my camera bag. "If I need to leave the building and come back, what's the code for the employee door?"

She told me the number. "Can you remember that, or do I need to jot it down for you, too?"

"No," I moved to the door and clutched the knob to wrench it open, "see you around."

First Gillian hated my guts, and now Chrissie Butane. I couldn't blame either one of them, really. But I walked the hell out of there fast before I lost my temper.

I headed for the elevators, walking by an employee pushing a dust mop through the aisles. The passenger elevator door was stuck open with a rubber doorstop. A make-shift barricade of packing tape suspended an *Out of Order* sign. Alternatively, a red arrow and block lettering painted on the wall directed me to the freight elevator. I moved over there, then skidded to a halt.

The latch clicked and the massive door lifted up. Two employees shifted out and began unloading an oak bedroom set. Turning around before I got in their way, I found the stairs and climbed to the top floor.

Reaching the last step, I paused to catch my breath. My chest heaved and my thigh muscles burned. That's what I got for shirking my daily workout routine the last couple of days.

To the right I found the storage room door. Pursing my lips, I noticed that someone had stuck an alarm company monitoring sticker on it to make the entrance appear protected. There was no lock.

"Cute."

I pushed the door open. A musty smell of antiques and old books swarmed my sinuses, like tufts of pollen on a spring day. Coughing, I turned my face away and rubbed my nose.

I crossed the threshold. Feeling along the wall for a light switch, I flicked it on. A single bulb mounted horizontally above the door illuminated the cluttered surroundings. The low wattage cast a lonely ambience. I waited a minute for my eyes to adjust to the dark.

The storeroom was filled to the rafters with forgotten relics from another century. Boxes stacked too high leaned precariously. Pieces of broken furniture were lined up against the walls. A harp with no strings jutted out from the far corner. A draft blew through a massive spiderweb suspended between beams in the ceiling. The silk strands expanded and contracted to the rhythm of slow breathing. And what was with the piles of mannequin body parts?

At least someone had shown a little good sense to maintain a path through the death trap. I followed the narrow walkway around a stack of boxes. Reaching a junction, I looked left then right. All of the windows to the left were blocked. I shuffled in the other direction where a faint strobe of light flashed through the windows.

The toe of my boot nudged something. I heard a metallic snap. A wooden plank shot upward at knee level, tumbled to clatter on the hardwood floor.

"Shit!"

Looking down at the ground, I spotted the rat trap

I'd tripped. Crumbles of moldy cheese speckled the weathered surface.

"Thanks for telling me about the traps, Chrissie," I muttered, making a mental note to watch out for more of them.

As I resumed heading toward the view, my elbow bumped a stack of boxes that reeked of old paper. The box on top toppled over and with no lid the contents spilled out. Ancient dog-eared and yellowed paperbacks scattered everywhere. In the event of a fast getaway, I needed to keep the pathway clear. Setting my bag down near the legs of a sawhorse, I kneeled down and picked up the pulp fiction novels.

The last one I grabbed to put back in the box was *My Gun Is Quick* by Mickey Spillane.

Standing back up, I moved deeper into the estate sale from hell. I passed a network of water pipes. The armless body of a female mannequin played sentry, tied to the vertical standing pipe with wire. Mannequin heads dangled from fishing line nailed to the rafters near the windows. Gusts of wind whistled through a broken pane.

I peered outside. Mother Nature was conducting an orchestra. It befitted a prelude to the apocalypse. Sheets of rain were her string section, strumming away on a mood of desperation. A flash of thunder rolled, lighting up the night in a diffused haze.

A brief power surge plunged me into darkness.

Knees bent, I scooted a pair of sawhorses back-to-back. Hefting a length of plywood, I set it down across the top of the sawhorses, perpendicular from the windows. Someone had drilled, screwed, and bolted a female mannequin head into the wood.

I set my bag of stakeout gear down by the bald head. Pulling the tripod out of the handles, I extended the legs, and placed them sturdily in front of the wide view. Something I saw on the floor made me to stop.

Squatting down, I fingered the recent prints of tripod feet in the dust left behind by someone else. A creaking noise came from behind. My skin tingled. It could've been the structure settling from the colder weather setting in. The creeps got the better of me.

I was glad Leslie had talked me into packing a gun, after all. I drew the .357 revolver from an ankle holster, then rose up, slowly. After looking around, I set the gun down on the make-shift workbench.

I mounted a video camera on the tripod. Next, the HP laptop came out, along with my new cell phone. I found an outlet below the window. Plugging the obsolete computer in, I tilted the screen up. While waiting for the hard drive to warm up, I took in the view to evaluate how well it covered my subject.

I could see the entire street and the east face of the vacant warehouse. The lights were out. Picking up the camera body, I screwed the 300mm telephoto zoom lens on. As I hefted the DSLR, I crooked my elbows to hold it steady, focused, then panned around the ground level of the structure. I couldn't find an entrance, but a pair of hinges and the seam of a door revealed a fire exit. Further down sat a couple of dumpsters defaced by coats of gang tags.

The handset chirped, sounding like an old-school Nintendo video game. I set the Nikon down on the workbench. Leslie's number appeared on the caller I.D. display.

"Hey partner," I answered. As she began to reply, static garbled her words. "Leslie . . . ?"

"Hold on. I'm here. The sound equipment must be interrupting my signal."

"Where are you?"

"Blush," she said. "Figured I'd start here because it was the last place where you had any contact with our clients. I've been listening to the greatest hits of mullet rock for over an hour. More than I've heard all my life. This place is a dump."

"Any sign of Mercer?" I asked.

"No. I've shown his picture around, too, and a number of dancers and the bartender didn't recognize him."

"Alright then, I'll talk to you in an hour. For your next stop, try Raw Assets." I told her what the clerk at 7-Eleven had said about the stripper with the stage name Star buying all their pre-paid smart phones. I also gave her the employee door code for the furniture warehouse to make our rendezvous later a lot easier.

"Not so fast, Matt. Give me the status from your end."

"Are you kidding? I'm stomping my feet in an old garment factory to keep my ass warm."

"Next time, wear your long john underwear like I told you," Leslie said.

"Easy for you to say," I said, my breath coming out in chilled puffs. "Since . . . "

"I get to hang out all warm and toasty with a bunch of naked chicks and you don't, nyah-nyah." She ended the call.

Movement snatched my attention; I glued my eyes to the lime green Honda Civic that pulled up alongside the warehouse. The fine-tuned engine hummed before it revved up, then cut off.

The rain stopped. I'd hoped that it would've cleaned the glass I was watching through, but the rain only loosened the sludge and made the view grimy. Flashing a look around the windowsill, I spotted a lever and turned it counterclockwise. A row of panes tilted open.

Snatching the Nikon, I checked the settings and

made damn sure the flash was off and that the ISO was on automatic. I didn't mind a little static in the photographs as long as the camera shake didn't fuck up the exposure, or a burst of light blew my cover.

I couldn't shake off the thought that I'd seen this exact car before. The driver's side door opened. Leaning forward, I hunched over, and brought the camera up to shoot. I bumped the viewfinder hard. The tissue around my eye was still inflamed from the brawl with Mercer.

A blunt pain swarmed around my head. My eyes filled with water. Clutching the camera to keep from dropping it, I pursed my lips shut to keep the curses of pain quiet. The grumbles I swallowed reverberated in my chest.

After shaking my head to clear a few stars, I brought the Nikon back up, and peered through the viewfinder (gently this time). The driver tossed a wrapper out, then closed the door. The engine cranked on. Pulling a tight U-turn, the street racer sped north. I held the shudder down, snapping five frames a second.

With a slow twist of my hips, I panned back over to where the Civic had parked, then zoomed in on the garbage the litterbug had discarded. The foil wrapper from a condom made me jealous as hell. If I wasn't stuck at this stakeout Ali and I would be getting it on right about now.

I stared at the deserted street for a good five minutes, trying to remember where I'd seen that ugly car. Giving up, I munched on a handful of trail mix. I found a metal stool to sit on. A thermos lid full of ice chips to suck on helped me think.

The lime green Honda Civic made me think about Pepper, only I couldn't figure out why.

Crunching the last chunk of ice, I grabbed the deck of cards from my bag. I unfolded the pack, shuffled the cards. I laid down a game of solitaire on the workbench. The illustrations of naked Suicide Girls on the cards sure made the game more engaging.

I focused more on the curves than the cards, losing three games in a row.

I heard a loud bang sound in the street. Hopping down from my perch, I looked outside. A transient had opened one of the dumpsters and was climbing inside. He proceeded to sort through the trash. The odor was pungent enough to waft upward into the storeroom. Wrinkling my nostrils, I shut the window.

A check-in call from Leslie was long overdue. The worry rising in me drew out each game. I kept glancing at my phone in between every card I dealt to match on a row. I lost again.

Uploading the photographs to the laptop, I blew up the pixels in Photoshop to spur my memory. The license plate number came out blurred, but legible enough to decipher. I thought about running outside to bag the condom wrapper. Most people in a rush to have sex tear them open with their teeth. Another torrential cascade of rainfall discouraged that idea though. DNA evidence would surely be compromised by now.

I reached into the bag of trail mix for a pretzel stick. An inch away from the crinkled opening my hand stopped. A cockroach the size of my thumb, its rear end dragging a larvae, skittered out.

"Gross. Disgusting."

Pile driving my fist into the tabletop, I tried smashing the nasty bugger. The roach scurried.

"That's right. Run you little shit."

It vanished over the back edge of the workbench.

I closed the bag of trail mix and stowed it away to dispose of later.

I considered texting Natty to see how she was doing, or calling Heather to provide an update on her case. She'd be able to run a check for the owner of the Honda Civic through DMV records a lot faster than I could. But I needed to keep the line open for Leslie.

Pulling my Walkman and earbuds out, I only inserted one bud so that I could listen for anything else outside. I turned the radio on and tuned in to KEX on the AM band. While working a stakeout, I'd listen to just about anything to flitter away the time, or to keep up to speed on current events. My favorite talk show came on.

"Listeners, welcome back," Mark Canon said. "Midnight is hours away and we've got plenty of explosive topics to chat about here on the Blast. Our next caller chases UFOs. Harley from Yuma, you're on the air."

In a cranky voice, Harley started to go off about aliens, conspiracies, and implants in his—

Long, staticky break ups began to interrupt his anatomical descriptions, creating dead air.

"Harley, turn off your radio," Canon urged. "There's a ten-second delay and you won't be able to hear yourself talk. Harley . . .?"

Canon hung up on the nut ball.

"Megan from Gresham you're on the air."

"How's Mason doing?"

Mason was Canon's pure-bread pit bull. His tone of voice dropped into a charming, smooth baritone.

"That's sweet, Megan. Thanks for asking. He's doing great. We went for a walk in the park this morning, played some fetch, and took a few pictures. I've posted a link on my website to my Instagram page. Speaking of my website, there's another link that I want everyone to consider clicking. The Skidmore House, a shelter in downtown Portland, needs our help. For years Skidmore House has operated as a Roman Catholic shelter that provides a haven for abused women. The Multnomah County Tax Assessment Office has ordered Skidmore House to pay a $50,000 property tax by Tax Day, or the building will be closed and sold to the Board of Human Services. Please, follow the link to their donation site, and help this institution of goodwill and safety stay open."

I smiled warmly at the shelter being mentioned. Maybe they stood a chance at raising the funds. Pepper had moonlighted there as a volunteer. We'd spent our first Thanksgiving together cooking up dinner for the staff and residents.

I still wanted to believe that there was more to Pepper than a cold-blooded killer.

"We're back on the phones," Canon said.

Through the next hour callers debated about various hot topics.

The United States should build a wall to block illegals from Mexico. Senators needed to pass stricter bans on firearms. President Obama deserved to be impeached for signing the Patient Protection and Affordable Care Act into law. Launch nukes on North Korea. Gentrification in Portland, San Francisco, and Seattle raising the cost of living so high that they now catered to entitled dot-com billionaires, instead of the middle-class citizens born there.

Canon moderated each conversation fairly and maintained his calm.

"Damn it, Leslie," I shouted. "Where the hell are you?"

"It's time for a bite to eat, folks," Canon said. "While I step away from the mic, here's an eclectic playlist of retro garage band hits to keep you occupied. First up is *Psychedelic Siren* by the Daybreakers."

Snatching my phone off the workbench, I dialed Leslie's number. It rang once and picked up, only she didn't answer. I could hear a bunch of men cheering in the background over an alternative beat. It sounded like Stone Temple Pilot's *Sex Type Thing*, an anti-rape grunge song Scott Weiland had written after his girlfriend was raped by three high school football players.

I turned the Walkman off to focus all my hearing on the call.

Some guy overloaded on testosterone yelled, "Take

it off! Woo-hoo, yeah!"

"Leslie . . .? Hello. Are you there? Leslie," I shouted, spraying the handset with what little spit I had.

I got scared for my partner. Although I knew her to be a capable and seasoned P.I. who could take care of herself, Mercer was no ordinary street thug. She wouldn't be able to take him down alone.

Still no response.

A woman's blood-curdling scream wailed. The connection went dead.

Shoving the phone in the back pocket of my jeans, I ran out of the storeroom, and barreled down the stairs two at a time.

TEN

Leslie Crow

Straddling a bar stool, I looked on as another stripper walked up on stage.

The smarmy voice of one of my foster mothers that'd tried to enroll me into the world of beauty pageantry seeped from my memory. 'Knees together, Leslie. A lady reveals nothing.'

At the time I was sixteen and insolent.

"I'm not a lady, bitch," I'd replied.

It gave me the proudest welt on my cheek that I'd ever worn.

The deejay excused herself to go on a break. Meaning I wouldn't know the stage names of the girls. I felt like I was wasting time, and I'd lost count of how many nude girls I'd seen. This tour of strip joints was turning into a job more aggravating and insulting than taking macro shots of lesbians having sex.

One of the dancers had worn a feathered war bonnet

for her set. It took all the restraint I possessed to remain seated when I really wanted to rush the stage and throttle the skank.

The latest stripper jerked her shoulders and the translucent nighty drifted to her platform-heeled feet.

Courtney Love snarled *Violet*. The angst and the beat reminded me of my twenties. Particularly when Matt and I first met. For a second, I pondered whether or not the rage in me had tamed since then.

She gyrated over to me. Hair short in the back showed off her graceful neck, while long bangs concealed her gleaming eyes. I thought it was amazing that her obstructed vision didn't cause her to trip. With a brief shimmy and shake of her assets, the stripper's full purple lips rounded up into a flirting smile. As the other guys catcalled dirty things about her body parts, I acted cool and just smiled right back.

I could never be a stripper. By now I would've been throwing drinks in faces or breaking noses.

In the mirrors behind the stage and mounted in the ceiling, I noticed a patron radiating more focus and reserve than me. A twenty-something Goth girl with red hair tossed a pair of ones on the rail. The twinkling lights bounced off the silver pyramid studs that lined the shoulders and pockets of her sleeveless blue denim jacket over a black tank. Scribbling on a tablet of sketch paper in her lap, the Goth only glanced up briefly to scrutinize details. She lowered the tablet enough for me to catch a glimpse of her chestpiece tat: the face of a wolf.

The stripper crawled over to the redhead. Rising up to her knees in front of the artist, the exotic dancer leaned in close.

Discipline as sharp as the wood pencil gripped in her fingers, the Goth continued to draw. She'd obviously seen sexy cleavage close up before. Her red lips pursed in concentration, stroking the graphite along the thick paper.

"Let me help you," the stripper said, her arms twisting behind her back to undo the clasp. She yanked the blue Latex bra off and flung it over her shoulder.

The stageside crowd went wild with louder wolf whistles and howling. My entree of steak bites had gone cold. I'd only bought them to make the efficient waitress for this section leave me alone.

The fella in a corduroy blazer sitting to my left tapped a finger on my shoulder.

"Excuse me, miss," he said. "I noticed you're not eating those. Mind if I . . ."

I slid the heaping plate of grass-fed beef, along with the fork on a cloth napkin and the A-1 sauce, his way. "Help yourself."

"Thanks. Can I buy you a beer or a salad?"

I flinched, taken aback. His courtesy sounded genuine, not like a pick-up line. Glancing at the salad bar located too close near the main stage for my liking, I shook my head.

"Just a Coke will be fine," I said.

My voice went unheard. The stout patron shoved

a bite of steak into his mouth. He chewed my food, waggling his head with the tempo of the short-haired stripper's double Ds that swayed in his face.

Gold stars were inked around her hardened nipples.

I looked back at the Goth's reflection in the mirror. She'd forgotten to peal a visitor sticker off the front of her jacket. Straining my eyes, I was able to make out the insignia of the Portland Police Bureau.

The stripper's second song started. Stone Temple Pilot's *Sex Type Thing* surged a wave of lust. She slinked around the stage in her thigh-high stockings, fueling the frenzy. She showed a lot of courage, flaunting her body to a song about control, violence, and abuse.

The sketch artist jumped to her feet, scowling as if the performance had hit a raw nerve. She stomped away.

I slapped a twenty-dollar bill on the counter. My iPhone vibrated. Reaching for the inside pocket of my duster, I took the handset out and tapped the screen to silence it. *Not now, Matt.* The dancer pranced my way.

Draining his bottle of lager, the patron on my right stood up. The lights shined off his bald head, the row of steel hoops in his ears, and the frames of his octagonal, copper eyeglass frames. Ever since he'd sat down beside me he'd been jotting down notes in a leather-bound journal.

"Novel deadline awaits," he mumbled, then vanished into the crowd.

The stripper kneeled down. Hopping over the railing, her knees skidded across the counter. Bracing her

right hand on the vacated stool, she swung her athletic legs down and rested her left knee on the cushion.

"A nice tip like that gets you more than just a look," she said.

Removing the picture from my duster pocket, I flashed Mercer's profile.

"I just need you to look at this photograph. Have you ever seen this asshole before?"

She brushed her bangs aside with her free hand. Eyes widening the size of cherries on a slot machine, the stripper let loose a high-pitched shriek of terror.

Jackpot, I thought.

Before I could reach a hand out to try and calm her down, Star bolted.

Hopping off my seat, I spun around to pursue her.

She knocked a server down. A tray of beer bottles, pints filled to the rim with brew, and a goblet of wine flew up everywhere above a crowd that'd formed to near capacity. The glass smashed into the counter in front of the vacant stool. Glass shattered and the liquid red as blood splashed the stage. Patrons wearing booze instead of drinking it yelled, flinging curses at each other. Gripping the edge of table, the waitress pulled herself up on wobbling legs. She whipped a towel out of her apron and moved to wipe spilled beer off a patron's bulging shoulder. The dickhead shoved her back. Careening off balance, the waitress's boobs struck the back of a chair. Groaning in pain, she hit the floor.

A pair of bouncers dashed in to contain the

disturbance before it turned into ugly pandemonium. One helped the server, and the other grappled with the dickhead as he decked another patron.

Head down, I darted through the melee. Catching sight of Star pushing through a pair of her co-workers, I slowed to a trot. A pint glass struck the floor at my feet. Crystal shards scattered. A sign above the double door Star escaped through read *Private*. Trampling through the suds, I resumed the chase.

The two strippers just stood there, taking in the spectacle. I shoved them apart to squeeze past.

"Watch it, bitch," one of them shouted.

"Get the fuck out of the way," I shouted back in a staccato rhythm.

The door at the end of the hall on the right slammed shut. I heard a cheap lock click.

Banging on the door with a fist, I cried out, "Star, I'm here to help you. Don't run."

An emergency exit door alarm on the other side blared.

Stepping back, I planted a firm kick beneath the doorknob. The latch held. I kicked the shit out of it again. The wood splintered. I kicked once more, pissed off.

The entrance to the dressing room flung open.

I sprinted between beauty mirrors and a bank of lockers. Clearing the fire exit door, I ran alongside the rear of the building to the parking lot. I saw Star in a slick leather trench coat sashed tightly around her wasp waist, running barefoot on gravel. She jumped into a

2005 metallic gray Pontiac Grand Am and sped off.

Dashing over to my car, I deactivated the alarm in mid-stride. I bumped my head climbing into the driver's seat. No time for pain to hurt or to slow me down, I started the Saturn with a wrenching turn of the key. Disengaging the emergency brake, I shifted into drive, then raced out of the lot before the cloud of dust and exhaust fumes from Star's getaway dissipated.

I turned north onto McLoughlin Boulevard. Peering out into the night, I spotted the Grand Am's taillights shrinking in the distance. As Star swerved around the double line to pass a vehicle, I repeated the Grand Am's license plate number out loud to myself over and over, till I memorized it.

●

Dialing Matt's new number, I wanted to let him know what happened and that I was en route to Stumptown Liquidators. The generic voicemail greeting answered. I turned west onto Stark, then double backed a few blocks south. The parking lot for Pearl Oyster was packed. I could smell the aromas of their Creole cuisine.

After I circled around the neighborhood blocks two more times, I gave up and parked in the loading zone behind the furniture warehouse. I cut the engine. A shiver trickled down my spine.

Star's Grand Am was parked at the end of the street near the southeast corner of the vacant warehouse Matt's new detective friend wanted us to stakeout. All the car doors were closed and the engine was running.

I didn't see any heads inside. If they were laying down their breathing wasn't fogging up the windows, yet.

Reaching under the seat, I withdrew my gun belt, and jutted my waist out to strap it back on. While visiting the strip joints, I'd kept the belt hidden away because the metal detector sweeps at the door would've picked up my pistol.

I stepped out of my car. A survey of the street revealed it seemed deserted. The exhaust puffing out of the Grand Am's tailpipe polluted the air. Walking by Star's ride, I peeked through the windows and looked for any signs of foul play.

Nothing.

Turning right, I reached the main entrance double doors of the warehouse. The chain and padlock dangled from the right handle. Whoever had unlocked the entrance seemed to be in a hurry. They didn't bother to shackle the lock to prevent someone from running off with it.

At least the lights in the building were already on, making my search for Star a little easier.

I drew my Glock. Parting the left door open with my foot, I moved inside. The gun in a two-handed grip, I cleared the right corner behind me. The lens of a defunct surveillance camera stared at me. Smooth as the wind, I swiveled around and patrolled the rest of the area.

Party confetti littered the ground floor. Two stacks of packing crates, each one about half-a-story high, sat in the center along the north wall. Behind those were a lineup of offices. The lights for those rooms were off, except the one in the northeast corner.

Bringing my pistol up, I approached the illuminated room.

The door opened. Star stepped out. She saw me aiming the gun at her head and gasped.

"Please, don't shoot."

I holstered my sidearm.

"I'm not here to harm you," I said, skipping up to her, "I'm here to protect you."

"Who are you?" Star asked.

"I'm a private eye. Come with me. I'll get you someplace safe."

A deep laugh echoed all around the room. My ears told me the source came from behind me. Whirling about, I aimed the Glock upward.

Distracted by the office spaces, I'd neglected to search the stairs, which lead to the mezzanine that wrapped around the entire building between the ground and second floors. My eyes locked on the target I'd been hunting for all night. Antonio Mercer's mouth contorted into a vicious grin.

"So, you're the American Indian P.I. that killed one of my men in San Francisco. I thought you'd be taller."

Mercer's calming voice belonged on a jazz radio station that lulled listeners to sleep. Knowing that this asshole had beat the shit out of my partner let me know that wasn't going to happen.

"If you're pissed about your man getting lead

poisoned," I said, sidestepping toward the crates, "take it up with the albino. He didn't have to get his gun off in a back alley."

I released a hand from the gun butt and motioned Star with a wave to stick close to me. But she just stood their like a deer in headlights, looking up at the sound of Mercer's voice like she'd been hypnotized.

"Star," I snapped.

Finally, she noticed my signal and followed my lead.

"True," Mercer said. "Although, you didn't have to hold him up like a shield."

"You weren't there," I said.

"I'm a strategist, Leslie. I've ran militarist campaigns all over the world."

"Bullshit," I scoffed. "You're nothing but a henchman that sells his services to the highest bidder. You're a mindless thug for hire. At most, you're a private contractor that submits the lowest bid for the job."

Mercer's front profile metamorphosed from a gentleman's into that of a monster's.

"Your backwater town mind is meddling with a business that will bury you, just like the U.S. military slaughtered your ancestors," he said.

"Fuck. You," I said, then pulled the trigger.

Mercer ducked and the lights went out.

Dropping to one knee, I heard footsteps clanging on the mezzanine. I sighted up the barrel on multiple targets. The lights turned back on, but not in a fashion that I expected.

Half-a-dozen aim point lasers pierced the darkness to light up my body with red dots.

One bank of fluorescents above the catwalk directly ahead flickered on.

"Give me the journal and I'll kill you quick," Mercer said, his voice slightly muffled by the stock of an AR-15 rifle held snug against his shoulder.

His five men in tactical gear similar to his stood to his right and left, covering me in a kill zone from an elevated position.

"Drop the popgun, Pocahontas," the mercenary to my far right said.

"We'll discuss maintaining a civil tongue later," Mercer said.

"Stop toying around," the insubordinate mercenary said. "Let me do her."

A gunshot cracked. The sound waves of it bounced off the walls, pinged in my ears. The mercenary that defied Mercer clutched his throat where his body armor offered little to no protection. The stumbling corpse gurgled. His weapon fell to land on the deck. Tumbling over the railing, he smashed into the wood floor with a sound of crumbling bricks. After the impact broke his bones, the slain henchman moaned.

"Does anyone else want to question my authority?" Mercer asked of his men.

They responded with silence.

"Good. Leslie, I just killed one of my own men. He was my spotter in Iraq. Imagine how I'll make you suffer.

I'll ask you just one more time. Where's the journal?"

"I mailed it back to Ambassador Ivanovich," I said.

Mercer chuckled. "Nice try. You're too driven to be that careless, or stupid."

I shrugged. "You just murdered one of your own men to keep me alive."

"You're a tough woman to read, Leslie Crow. I respect that. At one point I even considered recruiting you and Matt Grudge into my organization."

"What stopped you?" I asked.

"The way you handled the case in San Francisco. We listened in to your conversation with the senator's gay son using a laser microphone from the rooftop across the street. I knew that I'd never be able to work with you after you did the 'right thing.' You gave the queer a choice."

The warehouse was getting cold. Goosebumps were beginning to sprout up on my hands and my neck. Beads of sweat were beginning to run down Mercer's forehead, though. What was making him run so hot. I raised an inquisitive eyebrow behind the sights of my gun.

"I've been poisoned," Mercer told me. "The butchers I work for didn't take kindly to the strippers that laundered their money stashing a hefty sum of it away for a rainy day."

As if on cue, rain began to beat the windows.

"After I deliver the journal and the money," Mercer said, placing his hands on the railing to lean forward and cough, "my employers will give me the antidote. If I don't receive treatment in twelve hours, I'll bleed out through every pore of my body like an Ebola victim."

"Tell me how the laundering setup worked," I said.

"You're not in a position to ask anymore questions, Leslie. Suffice to say, I'm a killer with nothing left to lose."

"Maybe I can help you locate the money," I offered.

"I'm way ahead of you," Mercer said. "Or, should I say, 'we,' Star?"

"I'm sorry, Leslie," she muttered, backing away from me. "After Ophelia's severed . . . " Star paused, her skin turning pale. "Tongue was sent to me by mail, I contacted Sphinx. She told me to meet her at a drug house in Northeast where she grew up. I walked in on Mercer's men restraining her as he injected a syringe full of heroin into her arm."

A clash of thunder rattled the stripper's shoulders.

"We made a deal," she said. "You and the journal for the money and my life."

"You stupid bitch."

"Don't listen to her, Star," Mercer said. "You're showing good sense. Now, where's the money?"

"It's gone," she said, swiping tears from her cheeks.

A diagonal bolt of lightning bisected the view through the windows. Sparks flew, the building or a transformer sustaining a direct hit.

"Kill them both," Mercer shouted.

The power went out, engulfing all of us in the

dark. I rolled behind the protection of the crates. As the emergency generators kicked on, the backup lights cast a dim glow. Rifle fire punctuated the atmosphere. Bullets ripped a stripe up Star's torso. Twitching, she flopped onto the floor and bled out.

I barged through the office door across from me in desperation. Gunshots shredded the frame into toothpicks. Hunched down, I charged for the emergency exit like a football player running for a touchdown. Shouldering the crash bar, I dug my heels into the sidewalk outside, and spun around for cover.

Sneaking a look back, I extended my Glock. A shadow with green lights for eye sockets lumbered towards me. Without hesitation, I squeezed the trigger. The hollow point rounds penetrated the night vision goggles, pedals expanding inside the wearer. Arterial spray spritzed the air.

I made a beeline for the northeast corner. The smile I gave my car drooped into a frown. The Saturn's tires had been slashed. Realizing that the lightning strike had knocked out the power all over neighborhood, I hurried into the natural cover.

The double doors to the bistro opened. Candlelight flickered inside. Their generator must've failed. A bouncer and a waitress were beginning to usher patrons out with apologies.

I blitzed by the front of the building, waving my pistol.

"Get the fuck back inside!" I shouted. "Get down!"

Quickening my pace, I ducked passed a newspaper kiosk and a tin storage box wheeled against a telephone pole at the southeast corner. The bouncer shoved people back inside. A parking valet hit the deck. His nose crackled against the concrete.

Large-caliber rifle fire blasted at my ass.

I heard bullets penetrate metal, ping through glass, and ricochet off the asphalt. People were screaming from the mayhem. The valet's station absorbed multiple hits. The lid popped off, and keys rained all over my head. Wood chips the size of matchsticks flew into my hair. I leapt sideways behind the corner.

A round nicked the edge. Jagged brick and mortar fragments scraped my cheek. Adrenaline helped with ignoring the pain.

Dropping onto my haunches, I caught my fleeing breath. Inside three seconds, a mercenary rounded the corner right on top of me, aiming his weapon high.

I jammed the barrel of my Glock into his ribs. The muzzle pressed against muscle and bone between the straps of his body armor. I squeezed off three shots. His momentum pitched him forward, while the point-blank range barrel rolled him in mid-air.

Digging my heels into the blacktop, I shoved off the side of the building. I darted into the parking lot jammed with cars. My instincts pushed me through a maze of chrome and steel. I jagged between mid-sized pickups and Range Rovers. A military-grade boot crossed an intersection ahead. I skidded to a stop, aimed my Glock at twelve o'clock.

With my head slightly tilted, I listened to the wind. The mercenary chasing me through the maze was a mouth breather. As I doubled back around an SUV, I saw his distorted reflection on the mirror-like surface of a Humvee. He was about to run right into me at ninety-degrees on my right. I holstered my weapon; I needed both hands to take him hand-to-hand.

I stuck my leg out. Arms sprawling, the mercenary flew forward. His rifle slid underneath a Corvette. He tumbled up to his feet, pulled a serrated knife from his belt.

"Have a taste of this, bitch."

As he swung the blade, I ducked and grabbed his arm. Swinging my legs upward, I twisted around to set the bottoms of my thighs on his shoulders. I gritted my teeth. A momentary sting sliced through my skin mid-calf.

I ripped a knife of my own from a sheath inside my duster, and stabbed all four inches into his throat. His jugular punctured, blood sprayed against windshields.

He dropped sideways onto the front of the sports car. We dented the hood on impact. Our combined weight triggered an alarm. The shriek would tip Mercer off where to start looking for me.

Rolling a handkerchief from my duster pocket up, I tied a tourniquet around the gash in my leg, and hoped it gave Mercer and his last man less blood drops to follow. I redrew my Glock and headed east in a limping jog.

ELEVEN

Matt Grudge

Running lights—yellow and a couple red—made me feel like I had broken a speed record to arrive at Raw Assets. After paying a steep cover charge to get in, neither the bouncers, the bartender, nor the dancers I showed Leslie's picture to recalled seeing her. One of the bouncers recommended I check elsewhere, holding an icepack over his eye.

"What happened here?" I asked. "It seems less crowded than usual."

"One of the dancers went batshit crazy and stormed out," the bouncer moaned. "Stirred up a ruckus. I suppose a few of the patrons didn't appreciate the violence and left. It happens. No one had to visit the emergency room."

A waitress remembered seeing Leslie; she'd served her a plate of steak bites while she showed dancers a photograph. From her posture and body language, I sensed something was off.

"What are you leaving out?" I asked, hoping my concerned tone sounded sincere.

"You work in a strip joint for while, you know a bad egg when you see one," she explained, then took another tact. Maybe she saw my jaw tightening with frustration. "No, not you or your girlfriend, sweetie. The last dancer she talked to. The one that ran out."

"Can you tell me anything else about her? She calls herself Star, yeah?"

She fidgeted and the glass she'd been drying fell and broke.

Two dancers on a break, a blonde and brunette, were sitting down at the other end of the bar, one reading Cosmopolitan, the other knitting a baby blanket.

"Leave her alone, asshole," the frigid blonde shouted.

"Listen! I'm a P.I. and I think my partner is in serious trouble."

"Whatever." The brunette didn't look up from her magazine. "If you're not here to buy a drink or a lap dance, fuck off. Hey, Walter. Turn the stereo on to AM 1190. They're playacting a cool mystery like *The Shadow*."

"You got it, beautiful." The human tank grabbed a remote control by the cash register. He turned the TV off and the receiver on to the Blast. He squinted my way, a look you see a lion give a zebra. "What are you still doing here? Beat it."

Mark Canon's monologue echoed from ceiling-mounted speakers.

"For you listeners just tuning in," he said, "my new caller is from the Pacific Northwest, where she is being pursued by an attacker and unable to get assistance from 911. Apparently, there's a blackout flooding them with calls? Lady, this is a news radio show, not a stage for you to pretend to be Orson Welles."

"Listen, you Art Bell knockoff—oh *shit!* He's spotted me," I heard Leslie gasp, and my eyes widened like a buck's caught in headlights.

"Hey, come on, we'll get fined for that. Lady? You there? Yup, another live one out there keeping Portland *weird.*"

I searched my back pockets for my burn phone. All my fingers found was a rip in the denim where the handset must've fallen out.

Barging out of the bar, I dashed through the nearly empty lot to my Impala, snatched the keys from my coat pocket to unlock the door, and fell behind the wheel.

I almost broke the key cranking the ignition. I turned the radio on and propelled my classic heap faster than my mechanic had warned it could take. As the needle climbed to eighty, I begged the radio for directions.

"Give me a street, Leslie," I said. My pulse raced along with hers.

"Okay, I've lost him for a minute . . . " Leslie panted to catch her breath. "The reason I called your show is because I'm hoping to God my partner is listening. We're a pair of private investigators—wait a second. The asshole's two blocks up . . . maybe he thinks I crawled through that window I broke?"

"Please, watch the language. Besides, why don't you just blow his head off with your heater, doll?" Canon asked through the side of his mouth, imitating Edward G. Robinson.

"Because he kicked it out of my hand when he surprised me, you fuck. I think it's safe for me to cross over to the next block. I'm going to an inner city gym near—" There followed a muffled noise, then a blunt slap. Leslie's transmission ended, but not before listeners heard the faint scrape of something being dragged.

I pointed the Impala back into the industrial network.

Spinning the wheel into a hard left turn onto Sixth Street, I felt the tires hydroplane. I bounced in the seat for added traction. More rain the size of hypodermic needles began to fall, giving the night doses of despair. Closing in on the youth center, the double entrance doors flew apart. Teenagers and staff came running out in a panic. I swerved left and right to keep from hitting them.

A guy in tactical gear stalked out after the dispersing crowd. He fired rounds from an AR-15 over their heads. When he noticed the front of my car zooming toward him, he adjusted the rifle muzzle. Ducking sideways behind the console, I heard three shots. Two perforated the windshield. Glass shards peppered my hair. The third went through the engine block and shredded the seat on the driver's side where my chest had been. I stomped the gas pedal. I heard a yelp and the car shuddered. Hitting the brakes, I turned the Impala ninety-degrees left. The dilapidated jalopy skidded to a stop with a jolt.

I considered getting Leslie's gun out of the safe underneath my seat, but I had no time. I jumped out of my car, got a crowbar out of the trunk, and sprinted to the front entrance.

The raggedy corpse of the mercenary I'd rammed with the Impala was bleeding out into a backed up storm drain.

I headed for the back across the gymnasium floor, kicking basketballs out of my path and found the flight of stairs leading to the roof. I climbed them two at a time, elbowed the unlatched roof hatch open, and stepped out to what would have been a panorama of downtown across the river—except the lights had gone dark.

"Turn around and lose the crowbar," Antonio Mercer said, the bark in his tone comparable to a rabid dog.

I gave the crowbar a toss.

Shaking Leslie by her throat with one hand, he stamped a revolver's barrel against her temple with the other.

I felt the muscles in my face tremble and tighten.

"I feel as if I've really gotten to know you and your partner over the last several months," Mercer said.

"You make it sound like we've been meeting for coffee," I said, my voice thick with disdain. "We're the good guys, you're the bad guy, and the only way you're getting off this roof is by having an accident."

His fingers tightened around Leslie's windpipe.

"Tell us where Ambassador Ivanovich is," she rasped, wriggling in his vice-like grip.

Appearing dumbstruck for a second, Mercer loosened his hand.

He didn't know about the abduction.

"Tell me who drives the lime green Honda Civic with a skull on the hood that resembles your special forces tat," I said.

Mercer squinted, weighing his options.

"The fucking sociopath did it," he said. "I warned him. Don't fuck with the U—"

Leslie butted her skull into the bridge of Mercer's nose while applying pressure to the nerves in his wrist. The .357 dropped from his grasp like a sizzling skillet. She kicked the gun in my direction.

I chased after it, but my footing slipped and I had to roll forward to grab it.

"Oh, shit. Matt!" I heard Leslie call out, then scream, her shriek reverberating between the converted warehouse and brownstone next door.

I came upright on one knee, weapon in hand, and cocked back the hammer before skidding around to aim it at Mercer.

He'd pitched Leslie over the side of the seven-story building. I could see her fingertips struggling for purchase on the brick ledge.

"Watch this." He waved his left hand. "Nothing up my sleeve, except . . . " Mercer's wrist flicked and a scalpel landed between his fingers, poised like a movie star's hand ready to sign an autograph. "Put down the gun."

"No."

"This little piggy . . . " Mercer cat-scratched one of Leslie's knuckles with the blade. She screamed in pain, then cursed. "What's it going to be, Grudge? Or does the next piggy go to the morgue?" He leaned forward to make a precise, deeper cut through Leslie's flesh and bone.

I stood up, holding the weapon by its snub nose. I gave my knees a couple swipes with my gloved palm while managing to narrow the distance between us. He grabbed Leslie's right wrist and pressed the blade to the veins raised up under her skin.

"Close enough," he said.

I tossed the .357 underhanded, putting too much into the throw so the weapon went over the side. His manic glare shifted from me and followed the Magnum till it clanged somewhere on the street below.

"Asshole, that gun was a gift," he was saying, then stood up from Leslie to turn around—right into my foot.

I kicked the scalpel out of Mercer's hand and hurried to pull my partner up. Clutching a forearm, I heaved, the tip of her nose just above the edge.

"Watch it!" Leslie shifted her weight and pulled me down lower.

He'd recovered the implement and swung it at the back of my neck, slicing the top of my hair. The strike left him open for the kick I drove into his groin. It backed him off long enough so I could make sure Leslie got a hand hold. As I spun around in a half-crouch alongside the ledge, I ducked under a throat-level swipe, caught his wrist, then locked him in an arm-bar to wrestle the scalpel upward.

While Mercer grunted to overpower me, I squeezed the nerves in his left wrist. The scalpel dropped over the side.

Mercer rammed my hip with a soccer striker's knee, boxed my ears, then followed through with a forearm bash across my neck. He pulled me onto my back, kicking my ligaments in. I watched his boot heel dropping toward the bridge of my nose.

Rolling backward, I braced for a handstand, curving my legs up and over to slam Mercer's chest with both feet. He staggered back, flung off balance, then his tailbone absorbed the impact with the ground. It gave me enough time to stagger to my feet for round two.

I came out swinging. A backhand dislocated Mercers's jaw, and an uppercut to his chin made a molar fly. I winced, clutched a spurting wound in my bicep, and whirled away from another scalpel in Mercers's right hand.

He stepped up onto the ledge opposite the one Leslie hung on, taunting me with his scalpels to follow. Sweating fear, I stepped carefully onto the narrow space. He slashed at my mouth with one of the surgical blades. I leaned back, waving my arms for balance. Below us I spotted a fire escape, caution tape wrapped and hanging around its railings. Then I was ducking under a combination of stabs, finally driving a punch into his gut.

"That's it, Grudge. Let's continue to beat each other to a pulp while your partner holds on for her life."

It was his turn to laugh; a cruel and sadistic sound that made me wonder if that's what a clown on crack sounded like.

Rising from a crouch, Leslie blindsided Mercer, bashing his ribs in with the crowbar. He tumbled down onto the fire escape's top landing. Disoriented, he stood, tripped, and rolled out of control down the flight of steps to the next level.

"Shit, I forgot that was down there," Leslie commented with a vengeful sneer.

An oncoming semi's headlights illuminated his pulverized face and the mess of swollen bruises and red knuckle marks. We watched him stagger upright and start to haul ass down the fire escape, oblivious to the simple physics about to intervene.

Every bolt fastening the fire escape to the rear face of the youth center popped away. Mercer screamed as the faulty escape descended toward the truck, its horn blaring the driver's alarm. The semi's grill rammed the twisted metal to which Antonio Mercer clung, separating all the bones in his body from his vital organs, spattering crimson over the windshield.

EPILOGUE

Matt Grudge

Fog swirled outside the bay windows of Southeast Grind, a twenty-four/seven coffeehouse on Twelfth and Powell. Gamers and students typed feverishly at their laptops. Espresso machines hissed and poured. All walks of life stopped by or stayed awhile to satisfy their caffeine fix.

Leslie and I were breathing in the bold and savory atmosphere. It seemed an ideal place to get some work done on a lazy Sunday morning, and proved useful for meeting clients that wanted their interactions with a pair of private eyes to be a little more discreet than an office visit.

"What's wrong with you?" Leslie asked, moping

herself.

Green Beans had changed owners. It compelled us to hang out in another coffee shop.

I was watching the barista with honey blonde hair at the counter. She flashed me an occasional smile. Gold loops in her glossy lips glinted.

Looking at Leslie, I regarded her with a slight frown. "I'm still curious who Mercer worked for."

I'm such a liar.

The barista's attention was making me wonder if I could ever become a one-woman man.

A week ago, Halloween night, Ali had gotten a phone call while we were watching a horror flick marathon. After the call ended, Ali jumped around her condo and squealed in delight like a high school sophomore asked out to prom. She'd been offered a job managing a vegan food cart.

One of the perks included building a brand-new menu using nothing but local and seasonal ingredients. I hadn't seen her all week. Her absence was making me horny as fuck.

"Let it go, Matt. The Ivanovich abduction case is out of our hands. The F.B.I. seized Ursula's journal. Ambassador Ivanovich is still missing, probably dead. They would've heard about a ransom demand by now."

"Closed, huh? Really . . . " I said, rising up out of my chair a few inches to look over and down at her tablet screen. I saw the digital copy of Ursula Ivanovich's journal she'd made, and was marking up with characters and symbols. "We should take a trip to the library. Maybe we could find the key there."

"Ivanovich's head of security, Peter, reached out to me," Leslie told me. "He said that he'd like us to continue pursuing the human trafficking connection. He still believes that even if the Feds locate his boss, they'll likely cover up any trace of the pipeline Ursula uncovered. I'm going to canvass the neighborhood near the Brooklyn Yard. Flash Ursula's picture to a few residents, see if any criminal activity linked to trafficking crawls out from under a rock."

"Have you talked to Gillian?" I asked, glancing at my laptop screen. I was compiling a brief about what'd happened for tax purposes, and in case the Feds pushed to suspend our P.I. licenses.

"Ever since her firm fired her for going to bat for us?" she said. "Not much. She texted me, mentioned she's moving back to Boston. She also asked me, as a personal favor, to dissuade you from calling her."

The barista brought me my breakfast sandwich on a jalapeño and cheese bagel loaded with fluffy eggs and extra-crispy bacon. Leslie ordered a green tea smoothie. I could see flecks of spinach and lumps of kiwi suspended in the frothy mixture. Setting two napkins down next to my hand, the barista tapped the one with a phone number jotted down on it.

"Call me," she said.

Leslie didn't bother waiting for the barista to float away. "I told Gillian that wouldn't be a problem."

"What's that?" I asked. "Huh?"

"Exactly," Leslie said, then took a drink of her concoction. She licked a green mustache off her upper lip. "Mmmm. Tasty."

We ate and worked on our mutual investigative tasks in silence for a while. I was staring at Star's obituary from the *Oregonian* I'd clipped out and scanned to include in the case file. Her real name was Linda Reynolds. She hailed from Austin, Texas. Even though the three strippers had hired Alternative Investigations under false pretenses, I felt like I'd let them down.

I could've helped them better, too, if I hadn't been so goddamn distracted by the angles and the curves at the strip joints.

"How do you think the money laundering operation at the clubs worked?" Leslie asked.

"I'm hoping that the guy we're meeting here this morning can confirm a suspicion I have about that," I said.

Tapping the mousepad, I viewed a blown-up JPEG image of the lime green Honda Civic's license plate number. I pasted it to the file. Pressing the right arrow key brought up a PDF document of a registration form, courtesy the DMV. The Oregon driver's license of the new suspect connected to Mercer and the strippers laundering setup materialized.

I really didn't give a shit who Mercer worked for. I wanted to know who had the balls to hone in on the psychopath's territory. Mercer was hoodwinked.

"Excuse me," a buff man with a salt-and-pepper goatee and flattop said, standing over our table. "Are you Matt Grudge? I thought I recognized you. I've seen you before at Natty's place."

I stood up, and so did Leslie. Not only was our urgent appointment standing up on crutches, he was flanked by two little girls wearing lengthy black braids. They were adorable.

"Yes, yes I am," I said, shaking his hand with a tight clasp. "And this is my partner, Leslie Crow. Thanks for coming here to meet with us this morning, Bryan."

He shook Leslie's hand and smiled.

"No problem," the bouncer said. "Anything for Natty."

Pleasantries out of the way, Leslie packed up her stuff. I closed my laptop and tucked it underneath my arm. I gestured to a private room off to the side of the establishment, which I'd reserved in advance.

"Would it be alright if I got your girls some hot chocolate while you and Matt talk?" Leslie asked.

"With marshmallows?" the tallest of the pair said, her green eyes widening.

"Now sweetheart," Bryan said to his daughter, just a hint of scolding in his voice, "we don't ask for more when we're offered a treat."

"Sorry, daddy."

"If it's okay with Miss Crow, I'm alright with it. Just small ones, though. You two still have plenty of candy leftover from trick r' treating."

"Right this way girls," Leslie said. "Tell me about your Halloween costumes."

I walked Bryan into the study room. Someone hadn't cleaned up after themselves, left a plate of crumbs and a mug on the table. I set my computer down, then bussed the table. By the time I returned with a cup of black drip coffee for Bryan, he was already leaning his crutches against the wall behind him, and sitting himself down.

"What happened?" I asked as I shut the door.

"Oh, nothing serious. Took a knife in my thigh while covering the door at Raw Assets the other night. I'm more pissed about my jeans needing cut open at the emergency room."

"Mind if I record this?"

"Not at all," Bryan said, taking a drink of his java. "That's good. Fresh. It's warm in here, though."

He rolled up the sleeves of his black-and-white checkered flannel shirt. His forearms bore roped muscle covered in black and gray tats of geometric patterns. Working as a prison guard and a bouncer kept him in rugged shape.

"So, what can I do for you?" Bryan asked.

I set a micro-cassette recorder down on the table, and clicked the Record button.

"On the night I surveilled ARDOR, I noticed you looking at the deejay sideways."

"David Helix."

"That's him," I said, looking at the deejay's license and registration for his Honda Civic queued up on my laptop screen. "Care to tell me anything out of the ordinary about him that you've observed? Have you ever seen any of the strippers behave around him differently?"

"He's a cocky little son of a bitch," Bryan said. "Don't get me wrong. He's a great deejay. Plays good songs, no matter what kind of gig he's organized, or under contract as a performer to entertain." Bryan scratched his head. "I just don't understand why that earns him so much in tips. And oftentimes, he doesn't even play a particular song that the stripper liked, but she still tips him anyway."

Turning off the tape recorder, I reached across the small table to shake his hand. "Thanks for the information. It helps me and my partner out a lot. Can I ask Natty to get in touch with you again if something else comes up?"

"Yeah, of course," Bryan said.

Bracing his hands on the edge of the table, he boosted himself up. He grabbed his crutches and hobbled for the door. I opened and closed it for him to leave.

I sat down. Leaning backwards, I collected my thoughts.

I'd finally remembered where I'd seen Helix's Honda Civic before it showed up during the stakeout. It had roared along Morrison Street when I was walking to visit Pepper, the night after Dee-Dee Magnolia was murdered.

Coincidence?

Opening Explorer, I brought up several news sites I'd bookmarked over the last week that reported on Heather's apprehension of the supposed Tabor Strangler rape suspect. I saved a picture of the crime scene. Photoshop enabled me to zoom in and sharpen what I needed to see. That street racer and David Helix had detailed the exact same skull on the hoods of their cars.

I pulled up Helix's financial records from last year, then calculated a few equations in my head. All those partygoers lined up around the block to attend one of his raves at twenty bucks a head. Looking at the multiple zeros behind his annual net income, I whistled.

Maybe I should've been a deejay.

I called Heather. Her voicemail answered.

"It's Matt. Call me as soon as you can. I've got information about a new suspect for your case."

AUTHOR'S NOTE
&
ACKNOWLEDGEMENTS

The road to finishing *The Grunge Operatives* has been a long and winding ride. I started developing and writing about Matt Grudge and Leslie Crow back in the late nineties. Nirvana and Pearl Jam were not played on "classic rock" radio. The first draft of this book failed miserably. My writer's voice lacked the life experiences to back it up. Late 2007, I felt pretty good about the second draft. I shopped it around at a Willamette Writers Conference. An acquisitions editor for Kensington Books agreed that the idea of a pair of grungy private eyes seemed marketable. But he also informed me that my prose needed work. The manuscript weaved too many plot threads into one book. I also had a problem with show versus tell.

I shelved *The Grunge Operatives*, and moved on to writing *Skin Deep Motives*, instead. A novella allowed me to focus on Matt and Leslie's characters, while the plot threads I reigned back in gestated. The events in *Skin Deep Motives* and *The Grunge Operatives* take place in late 2010. There's a reason for that. My stepfather, Earl Shea, passed away on Halloween night, 2010. Writing became a thing I depended on for survival and managing my grief.

As it continued to do through 2014 after my mom joined Earl. I hear grief described as coming in waves. Each page of this final draft kept me afloat. I even filled them from time-to-time with references to my parents. Maybe I'll mention them sometime at a book signing.

So, without further ado, special thanks to:

Alex Hurst for her energetic talents as an editor and wordsmith tightening the bolts of this story.

Daniel Cooney for rendering illustrations of the alternative world in my head, which always boosts my creativity if a block appears.

Simone Rene for her portrayal of Leslie Crow becoming my muse.

Dax Santi for capturing miraculous images of Simone through the lens.

Nick Slosser for his wise counsel assuring me not to rush in. Take my time. Savor the story.

Marg Gilks for her tactfulness and encouragement, which enabled my craft to enter a new phase of evolution.

And my readers for being patient while I finished this book. Stay with me. The journey is just getting started.

PARTNERS IN CRIME PUBLISHING

THE AUTHOR

A Portland native, Aaron Hilton has worked at a video store, in a mail room, accounts payable, security, and for the last eighteen years, as an alarm control operator for Fred Meyer and Kroger. He enjoys digital photography, film *noir*, pin-ups, scary movies, sequential art, and strong coffee.

He is currently working on the third book in the Alternative Investigations series, *A Dying Art*.

Photographer Credit: Angelique Herrington

THE EDITOR

Alex Hurst was raised in the wilds of the south. Lightning storms and hurricanes created the playpens of her youth, and in the summers, she used to spend all of her time dodging horseflies in a golden river, catching fish and snakes with her bare hands, swinging from vines, and falling out of magnolia trees. These days, she wrestles prose and courts typography as an author, editor, and book designer. She thinks the Grunge Operatives deserve their own TV show.

www.alex-hurst.com

Photographer Credit: Alex Hurst

THE ILLUSTRATOR

Daniel Cooney is the creator of the graphic novel series *Valentine* and the forthcoming graphic novel, *The Tommy Gun Dolls*, and the artist and author of the instructional books *Writing and Illustrating the Graphic Novel* and *The Complete Guide to Figure Drawing for Comics and Graphic Novels* published by Barron's. Cooney is a full-time instructor at the Academy of Art University and resides in Martha's Vineyard, Massachusetts.

Photographer Credit: Daniel Cooney

THE ART MODEL

Simone Rene originated from San Francisco. At the age of seven, Simone was enrolled in her first dance studio, focusing on ballet, lyrical and jazz. While attending the dance department at San Francisco School of the Arts, Simone befriended several visual art majors who found her dancer arms and legs ideal for art projects, which ignited her career as an art model. Simone's passion for art has expanded vibrantly; from graphic novels and video games to television. She's worked for Pixar, EA Games, Lucasfilm, and Crystal Dynamics. In the May, 2015 issue of *Xbox Magazine*, an image of Lara Croft she body modeled for splashed the cover. Simone is also an actress. Recently, she appeared in an episode of Major Crimes. To unwind after a hard day's work Simone loves cuddling up with her dog, Charlie Brown.

Photographer Credit: Colin Day

THE PHOTOGRAPHER

Born and raised in North Carolina, Dax Santi grew up influenced by artists. After studying sculpture and graduating from the Academy of Art University in 2005, he continues to study art through photography. He is the author of *Pinching Lobsters* and *High Tide and the Sandcastle*.

Photographer Credit: Alessandro Squitti

www.ingramcontent.com/pod-product-compliance
Lightning Source LLC
Chambersburg PA
CBHW050029180626
46810CB00002B/638